HOLIDAY WITH THE MYSTERY ITALIAN

HOLIDAY WITH THE MYSTERY ITALIAN

BY

ELLIE DARKINS

First published in Great Britain 2016
By Mills & Boon, an imprint of HarperCollins*Publishers*
1 London Bridge Street, London, SE1 9GF

Large Print edition 2017

ISBN: 978-0-263-07086-6

Our policy is to use papers that are natural, renewable and recyclable products and made from wood grown in sustainable forests. The logging and manufacturing processes conform to the legal environmental regulations of the country of origin.

Printed and bound in Great Britain
by CPI Antony Rowe, Chippenham, Wiltshire

For Matilda

CHAPTER ONE

'LAST BUT NOT LEAST, contestant number three, here's your question: As a gold-medal-winning ParaGames swimmer…' he paused for whoops from the enthusiastic audience '…I obviously spend a lot of time in the water. If you were a sea creature, what would you be and why?'

Amber suppressed an eye-roll. Seriously, this show couldn't be any cheesier if it tried. She had thought when she'd arrived that the flashing lights and tinsel-bedecked set were tacky enough, but this guy's titillating questions were taking the cringe factor to a new level. She just had to play along, she reminded herself, and get this over with. A charity gig was a charity gig, and when you worked in the media, even as a lowly newspaper columnist, you sometimes found yourself doing something completely embarrassing in aid of a kids' charity. Like appearing on a celebrity version of the country's best-loved dating show.

Luckily, with the answers she'd prepared, there was no way that this 'eligible bachelor' was going to pick her, even if the whole thing hadn't been scripted by the producers, so it was just a case of answering this last question, posing for a quick photo, and getting back to her laptop and her deadline. She still hadn't finished her latest column. Well, she hadn't actually started it yet—she had a mailbox full of 'Dear Amber' letters, and still had to choose the most interesting to feature on the magazine's website.

She took a deep breath and tried to remember the answer to the bachelor's final question that she'd written and memorised when she'd been emailed in advance.

'A killer whale,' she said, *sotto voce*. No doubt the man on the other side of the screen, not to mention the producers, had been hoping for something a little sexier. Something about mermaids and their shells and their penchant for handsome princes, or firefly jellyfishes lighting up the ocean. She'd considered several contenders for her answer, each designed to ensure that she would be the last contestant that this eligible bachelor would be interested in. ParaGames swimmer. That definitely rang a bell—Mauro someone. Welsh surname. She spent an hour every morning in her local pool, and had watched hours of footage of the international sports and para championships held in London a few summers ago. He'd won a clutch of medals, featured in a fly-on-the-wall documentary about his training regime and then been the face of various food and sportswear brands in the years since.

The voice too—she definitely remembered that: an unusual combination of Welsh and Italian accents that was unmistakable. Her brain flashed a pair of built arms, wide shoulders with droplets of water catching the light from a hundred flashbulbs.

She realised that the studio had fallen into silence around them, waiting for her explanation for her decidedly unromantic response. 'A killer whale,' she repeated, 'because they're intelligent, the women stick together and they can be ruthless predators when it's called for.'

For half a moment the silence in the studio stuck, but readers of her column knew what to expect from her. She called the shots as she saw them, and more often than not she saw the whole 'romance' scene as one big game that was rigged against fifty per cent of the players.

A deep, rich laugh from the other side of the screen stopped her train of thought, and she practically felt the noise flow through her, smooth and dark as the chocolate she kept permanently stocked in her kitchen. And in her desk. And in her bedside drawer just in case. Another flash of something from her memory. Hair slicked back and wet, a charming smile turned on a flustered television presenter. A shiver ran through her spine as she remembered the charm and the charisma that had exuded from this man, even down the camera from an echoing swimming venue. Good job she had sabotaged herself in this game. She had more than a sneaking suspicion that this man was going to be trouble for whichever unfortunate contestant got picked. She was best off out of it.

She sat cooking under the heat of the studio lights and looked longingly at the heaps of snow dotted around the studio. Sweat threatened to prickle at her brow and break through the industrial strength anti-shine powder she'd been caked with. Not that the polystyrene decorations would have helped much—but then there wasn't a lot of genuine snow around in September.

Due to 'scheduling reasons', they were filming this Christmas special in the autumn, and she had to admit that the fake festivities were messing with her mind. Christmas carol fatigue was an annual complaint, but she'd never suffered from it this early before.

Whichever contestant was 'picked' to go on this date would be summoned back in December for the live programme, when the footage they were shooting now, and the highlights of the date, would be shown.

As she waited for Julia to announce which 'lucky lady' had been chosen, she tried to think of the advice she'd given the woman in her last *Dear Amber* article, but the crash of the audience breaking into applause intruded into her thoughts.

The presenter announced, with a shake to her voice, 'And so it seems that our lucky contestant is Amber, a journalist from London!'

Amber wobbled on her stool as her jaw fell open. *Oh, please, no.* How could he have picked her? She'd said 'ruthless predator'! She'd not made a single sexual innuendo, no matter how leading his questions, not even the one about which swimming stroke was her favourite—

it had taken her an age to think of a response that didn't conjure images of breasts, butterfly kisses or caresses of a strong, muscled back. She knew for a fact that the producers had told him to choose one of the other women. Had he never seen this show before? He should be picking the person with the biggest hair—the one that the producers had pushed towards the most suggestive answers. She'd batted away their attempts to give her a makeover. She knew what she was working with, and a fake tan and big hair weren't going to change it. She glanced towards Ayisha, the show's producer, and from the look on her face it seemed that she was as shocked as Amber. It seemed that Mauro had just gone off-script.

She watched the two other women walk past the screen, and the groans of regret as Mauro met the women that he could be taking with him for their week in Sicily. Oh, God, a whole week with him. It had never even crossed her mind that he could pick her, and now she was signed up for a week-long holiday with a man that her brain had—goodness knew why—been stashing mental images of in a state of undress.

And then the music was rising to a crescendo and Ayisha was energetically motioning for her to get up. She took to her feet and straightened her spine, desperately trying to remember what they'd been told to do if they were picked. It had hardly seemed worth listening when she'd known that her prickly answers would keep Mauro well away. Keeping men at arm's distance was more than a habit these days: it was a reflex, as easy to her as breathing. Normally one flash of her 'don't even think about it' look was enough to have them backing away and leaving her alone, just as she liked it.

Perhaps that was the problem, she thought. He couldn't see her face, couldn't see just how desperate she was *not* to meet any sort of bachelor, eligible or otherwise. She stood on the spot where Ayisha had been gesturing and waited for the big reveal, her inner monologue not giving her a minute's rest in its utter contempt for putting herself in this situation.

The screen rolled back, with a wobble and a creak, and then she saw him, and realised she had been right. It was him, the athlete her brain had clocked and ogled, and then apparently saved half-naked images of in some deviant part of her mind, just in case it came in useful one day. His dark hair, not slicked back this time, but rebelling from a side parting, showed a hint of red—a dash of chilli hidden in the chocolate—and the shoulders dominated the rest of his body, making his waist look narrow, although she remembered abs that would make a lesser woman dribble. His wheelchair was small and space-age-looking, and the least interesting thing about this mountain of a man. An open shirt collar showed a triangle of tanned skin below his neck—and for just a moment Amber remembered that bronzed torso, thrust out of the pool by powerful forearms.

She shook her head. This should not be happening. He should not have picked the woman who had chosen her brain, when asked what her favourite part of her own body was. But the presenter of the show had grabbed her hand and was dragging her across to meet Mauro.

'Mauro, meet your date—Amber Harris. Amber, how do you feel to have been chosen?'

As if this was all a big joke, and she was the punchline. If he'd been able to see all three women she knew for a fact that he would have chosen one of the others.

'Erm…surprised,' she choked out, and didn't know whether to be pleased or not at the look on Mauro's face, the one that suggested that he liked catching her off guard, that maybe he'd done it on purpose.

'Well, Amber, just you wait until you see what we've got in store for you. You'll be jetting off on a romantic week-long break to sunny Sicily. Mauro has generously allowed us to use his luxury villa, complete with swimming pool, private beach and no fewer than seven beautiful bedrooms to choose from. Over the course of your week you'll be wined and dined by the owners of the Castello Vigneto, and tour the grounds of their beautiful vineyard before feasting on local foods and wines. You'll take jet-skiing lessons from Mauro himself, and can choose from any of the other water sports equipment available at his private pontoon. There will be a hike up the Mongibello, otherwise known as the live volcano Mount Etna, and to top it off we'll be flying you, by helicopter, to view the volcanic eruptions of the island of Stromboli! Amber, what do you say?'

Mauro watched Amber's shell-shocked expression as the presenter outlined the romantic week in Sicily that had been planned for his date. Well, he'd planned a large part of it himself, actually. When the charity had approached him about appearing on the show, he'd gone one better and offered the use of his home—it seemed to defeat the object of money-raising if they were to shell out on accommodation. And it was entirely unnecessary when he had his very own villa sitting empty most of the time. Anyway, as the patron of a charity that helped disadvantaged children through sport, he wanted to do more than just sign big cheques.

His villa in Sicily, the country of his mother's birth, was one of his favourite places on earth, so it was hardly a chore to spend a week there, especially a week in the company of a beautiful woman. Her blonde hair fell just to her collarbones in waves that seemed deliberately messy, and her eyes had grabbed his attention as he tried to work out whether they were more green or brown. But none of that was the reason that he'd decided to ignore the script the presenters had briefed him on, of course. Celebrity edition or not, he hadn't known who she was. The reason he'd picked her was simple: he'd been intrigued by her and wanted to know more. She was funny, for a start: he'd smiled at her answer to his first question, chuckled at her second and full-out belly laughed at her third.

And then there had been that attitude. The one that had said that she didn't for a second buy into the show's attempt at stirring up romance. The producers had told him that everyone involved knew that they were all just doing this as a money-raiser, that none of the women were actually interested in starting a relationship. But there had been one way to be sure that he wasn't getting involved with someone who had different expectations of this show from him—pick the woman that had Keep Out prickling her voice and written in neon letters so big he could see them above the screen that was keeping them apart.

She'd seen straight through his questions, straight through every pep talk and manipulation of the producers and refused to deliver the smut that *Holi-Date* had been leading her towards. She would have been a killer whale—who wouldn't have picked her after that?

She leaned in to kiss him on the cheek. Not exactly by choice—he was sure that he wasn't the only one who had instructions from the production team on what they were to do after the big reveal. What surprised him was that she was going along with it. The peck on the cheek was brief, gone almost before it started, but the scent of her shampoo, something earthy and familiar—rosemary, perhaps—lingered a second longer, teasing his senses. Two beautiful women had just sashayed past him—a singer from a girl band and a regular from one of the soap operas, apparently. But Amber... she marched. And though her expression wasn't quite a scowl, it wasn't the TV smile that everyone else in the studio was wearing either. No, she was definitely different. Good. Different was what he had wanted. Dating show or not, he wasn't in the market for a girlfriend, and no one had shown that they weren't interested in a relationship as eloquently as Amber had.

'And, Mauro, what do you think about your gorgeous date?' Julia, the presenter, asked him.

He took a moment to think about it. She was hot—there was no doubt about that. Slim legs were encased in dark jeans, and a hint of silk was revealed beneath her black blazer. The look was almost academic, it was so serious. And yet…something about it drew him in. Perhaps it was the thought of that silk, imagining the smooth warmth of it beneath his fingers if he managed to peel off that blazer, peel back the layers of protection that she had so clearly shown already that evening.

She hadn't given his chair more than a cursory glance—always a good start. Now she took a couple of steps back, guided by the presenter's hand on her waist, but her eyes hadn't left him yet. They'd dropped to his chest, he noticed, but they were making their way back up now, and…there. He had her again, her gaze locked into his. He wasn't going to let her go easily. He wanted to play with this—it wasn't as if he had to worry that she might want him to get involved.

'Oh, Julia, I'm very much looking forward to getting to know her better.'

Julia turned to the autocue and began to wrap up the show, but already he'd lost interest, could see only Amber as the audience were directed to clap and cheer. Then he realised he'd missed his cue. The two women were turning towards him and he realised they were meant to be making their way backstage. At this rate it'd look as if he was chasing Amber out of the studio—not the best of starts. He spun on the spot and caught up with her quickly then stopped at the mark they'd been given to turn and wave at the audience. He let out a breath of relief, and surprise. It took a lot to surprise him these days. He liked to think he'd seen it all—he'd spent the last ten years of his life *trying* to see it all in the wake of his accident. But somehow, after just half an hour in her company—and a large part of that without even being able to see each other—Amber had him chasing after her without his even realising how she'd done it.

He rarely had to chase. Normally, with women, he put in a little groundwork, a little charm; laid the bait and then waited for a bite. It never took long. Whether he was throwing a party, hanging out in a nightclub—hell, he'd picked women up in the supermarket—he always had this under control. He took advantage of every opportunity to experience something new, but always on the strict understanding that there was nothing more than a casual fling on offer. He didn't do commitment. Well, not to romance, at least. He was committed to his sport, his business, his charity work, and for ten years it had been clear to everyone involved that that didn't leave room for commitment to anything else.

As they headed back to the green room Amber kept her eyes dead ahead, and her shoulders seemed to stiffen and rise with every step that she took. Mauro hung back, nothing at all to do with wanting to keep an eye on that peachy *culo*, revealed with every swing of her jacket. But something about being close to Amber had made him concerned for her. That neon sign that had shown over the wobbly dividing screen looked different up close. There was hurt behind it, and a vulnerability that was making him wonder whether he had made a mistake in picking her. He had thought that it had been the straightforward, risk-free option, but now he wasn't so sure. He would give her space, he told himself. Space that she so desperately seemed to want.

She dropped onto the sofa in the green room and rested her head in her hands. Mauro moved in front of her and couldn't help but reach for one of her hands and brush it with his fingertips, before he remembered what he had told himself about giving her space. 'Hey, it's not that bad, is it?' he asked with a forced smile. It wasn't exactly flattering, that she seemed so traumatised at the thought of a date with him, but he knew from her answers on the show that this wasn't personal. She had had no intention of being the one to go on this date. He had thwarted whatever plan it was she had going on, and she was annoyed about it.

'I've made you angry?'

She looked him right in the eye.

'Maybe. Or maybe I'm angry at myself. I… It doesn't matter, anyway. Look—' she started gathering up her things, throwing her phone and bits of make-up into her handbag '—this has been…fun, and really nice to meet you and everything. But I've got to get back.'

'You're not staying for the party?' There were drinks planned—everyone on the show at a hotel in the city, where those from out of town were being put up. He wasn't staying at the hotel—he kept a penthouse suite in Mayfair for when he was in London—but it should be a fun couple of hours. From the looks he was getting from contestants numbers one and two he guessed that they would be at the party when he showed up. But for once the promise of a pretty face waiting for him in a bar didn't have its usual effect.

There was something about Amber that intrigued him.

Some of the things he'd worked hardest for in life had been the sweetest: his first gold medal the sweetest of them all. But with women…what could he say? He'd never had to work that hard. Women fell for him easily, and before things got too complicated, he got out. His life was too full, too packed with ambition and drive to fit in a relationship as well, but the board of the sports charity had assured him that just turning up for this date, making nice for a week for the show, would help their fundraising efforts no end. It didn't mean that he was here looking for a relationship.

He was so distracted by trying to work out what was really going on with Amber that he missed her moving towards him, until she was so close that he could smell that shampoo again.

Her lips brushed against his cheek, soft and plump, and he wondered what she would have done if he'd turned his head slightly, so that they touched against his own. So that he would have the taste of her on his mouth.

'I have to go. It was nice to meet you, Mauro.'

Something about the way she said it raised his hackles. Nice to meet him, but she wasn't planning on seeing him again, he thought. She was going to try and back out of their date. Well, he'd see about that.

CHAPTER TWO

AMBER TURNED UP to the airport with a fake smile plastered onto her face, her ears ringing with the warning her boss had just given her: go on this date or lose your job. OK, so it had been more nuanced than that, but that was what it came down to.

Recently, the feedback on her articles had been taking something of a dive. The comments on her online column had started off unpleasant and steadily descended into venomous. She'd stopped reading them, chalking them up to bullies with nothing better to do. But her boss had told her in no uncertain terms that the powers that be at the paper were paying attention.

And maybe they were right; Ever since her heart had been broken, she'd lost her home, and realised that the best advice she could dish out to anyone looking for romance tips was to get out, get your life together on your own, and make yourself happy. The words that had been bandied around in that meeting—cynical, bitter—when had she become that?

But how was she meant to undo the hurt and the anger that had been simmering under her skin? The pain that had become such a part of her that she wasn't sure if, never mind how, she was meant to shake it off.

This wasn't just about her feelings. If Maddie was right and her job was at stake...well, there was nothing that she wouldn't do to save her job. It was all she had. She'd literally lost the roof over her head when her relationship had broken down. Now her rent ate up most of her salary, and her travel card to get in from Zone Three took the rest. Even a month without work would be a disaster. She could *not* lose this job.

She'd thought she'd be able to beat the check-in queues by doing it online last night, only to be told at bag-drop that she had to go to the desk after all. It was taking an age—an immaculately manicured woman in an airline colours scarf was tapping at a computer and frowning at her passport.

'I'm sorry for the delay, madam.' She looked up and Amber forced her mouth back into a smile. There was nowhere she could escape the judgemental gaze of her readers. 'Some of the information from your passport was missing from the upgrade request, but it's all sorted now. Here's your boarding pass, and the executive lounge is just over there. Mr Evans asked me to let you know that he has already checked in.'

Executive lounge? With budget cuts at work, and the unmitigated disaster that was her personal finances, she'd got so used to travelling economy that she'd forgotten that there was any other way.

She determinedly ignored the flutter in the base of her stomach as she walked towards the lounge. There was no way she was going to allow Mauro Evans to have that effect on her. No way she'd be pulled into those sparkling green eyes and be tempted to flirt. The man was incorrigible—a playboy who was with a different woman on the front page of each week's trashy magazines, and remembering that was her best defence. She was sure that she was going to need one. She'd felt a pull of attraction from the second that she had realised who she was speaking to. A relationship, a fling, a flirtation was the last thing that she wanted, or needed. Especially with someone that the sidebars of shame told her regularly saw, conquered and came all in the space of a weekend. Every weekend.

Ugh, she didn't even know why she was worrying about this. It wasn't as if he was going to be interested in her. He had picked her for some perverse reason of his own. He must have wanted to annoy the producers of the show for some reason. Anyway, she had more important things to concentrate on.

She needed an image update. She needed her readers to see something different in her. Something that they could identify with. So far she'd been honest in her columns, brutally honest. But that wasn't what the readers wanted. *She* wasn't what the readers wanted. So while the cameras were rolling, she was going to have to be someone else.

Perhaps Mauro could help her out. No doubt he'd just gone into this whole thing looking for the image boost that came with charity work. She needed to show a softer side. Maybe there was a way they could both get what they wanted.

She didn't have to *do* anything. She didn't even have to promise anything. All she had to do was let the light of Mauro's brightly shining libido reflect on her for a while. All she had to do was be friendly.

When had that started to be something she needed to work at? Since when had friendly seemed like such an effort?

Her boss was right. Something had to change,

and a luxury holiday to a sunny destination—all on someone else's budget—seemed like as good a place as any to start a little soul-searching.

'Amber, you found us!'

Mauro greeted her as she stepped through the door to the lounge. He was already sipping from a glass of champagne, with the camera and a microphone pointed at him. The two members of the TV crew swung round at his words, and a camera was thrust in her face. She moulded her features once again into the smile that she'd practised in the mirror, and hoped that it looked more convincing that it felt.

'Mauro! This was a surprise. An upgrade?'

'The best way to travel,' he said with a smile, and the smallest salute from his champagne flute. 'Don't worry,' he added, and Amber guessed that some uncertainty had shown on her face. She'd thought that she'd kept her smile pinned in place, but he had seen through it. 'I matched the cost of the upgrade with a donation to the charity, if that's what you're worried about.'

Maybe she *should* have been worried about it. This was a PR exercise after all. But that hadn't been what she was thinking. What she'd been thinking was that his white shirt highlighted the hint of red in his hair and the golden warmth of his skin. That his hair looked as if it had been carefully undone, perhaps by some other woman's hands as he left her bed that morning. That the smile on his face was warm and open, as genuine as hers was strained.

'A great surprise, I should have said.' She forced the words out. 'Here's to the start of a great week.' Ayisha, the TV producer, had passed her a glass and she matched Mauro's toast with one of her own.

'To us,' Mauro said, with a searching look.

'To us,' Amber agreed, fixing her smile in place again, trying to hide the effect that Mauro was having on her.

God, he was attractive. Far too attractive for

his own good, or for hers. He had been sent to test her. That was the only way she could think of it. One week, trying to show a softer side. Showing that she wasn't the bitter old hack that the Internet had labelled her. But did the dating gods really have to send this guy to help? Someone who it seemed she was physically programmed to react to. Someone whose eyes seemed to twinkle into the depths of her own, who seemed to sense her discomfort, however hard she tried to hide it.

She sat beside him, and he reached for her hand, pulling her towards him for a friendly kiss on the cheek. A day's worth of stubble scratched her cheek—he'd lain in bed too long that morning perhaps. Had something more tempting than a close shave kept him there?

Good for him if it had.

Just because she was sworn off romance and men, and sex by default, that didn't mean everyone had to live her celibate life. If he was getting some, she was pleased for him, really.

And not in any way the teeniest, tiniest bit jealous. She settled into her seat and glanced at the screen showing flight details. Another hour until they had to be at the gate. Were they meant to make small talk until then? With the camera rolling?

'I think I might just have a look round the shops until they call our flight.'

She needed something to read, something to bury her nose in during the flight, to keep her eyes from wandering over to Mauro.

'Great idea,' Mauro said, draining his glass. 'Lead the way.'

'I meant—'

'You were trying to get away from me?'

He said it with a laugh, but the question in his eyes was serious enough.

'Of course not. I'm just surprised that you're so keen on shopping.'

'Casual sexism? I'm shocked at you, Miss Harris.'

She smiled, not quite sure whether he'd

shamed her or charmed her into it. 'Well, shopping it is, then. We'll meet you back here before we go to the gate,' she told Ayisha, pre-empting any thoughts of them following. She was going to have to get used to a camera watching her every move, of making sure that every word and action was projecting the image that she needed it to, but she couldn't just turn it on from nowhere. She needed to practise without the cameras on her. One misstep and she was sure that they would be all over her.

'So, then, what's it going to be?' Mauro asked. 'Handbags? Clothes? Are you going to disappear into the make-up for an hour?'

'Who's sexist now?' she asked. 'None of the above.' Her interest in make-up hadn't survived her relationship with Ian. She'd never seemed to get it right, however hard she'd tried—too slutty, too shabby, too colourful, too drab. In the end, she'd stopped trying.

She strode purposefully across the concourse towards the bookshop, dodging tourists dragging cases behind them with no sense of spacial awareness.

'What? My witty repartee isn't going to be entertaining enough for you?' Mauro asked as he zipped into a space in front of her, using his chair to clear a path through the throngs of holidaymakers. 'I'm clearly not making a great impression.'

'What can I say?' Amber replied with a shrug of her shoulders. 'I'm a writer. Which by default makes me a reader. We get a free pass to have our nose in a book whenever we want.'

'Even when there's something better to do.'

She laughed.

'Wow. I'm surprised you got that ego of yours in the terminal. And, for the record, I have absolutely no intention of *doing* you.' There, if she was going to try and flirt for the cameras then that needed to be said. She could pretend to be attracted to him now with a clear conscience. There was no leading him on if she'd already told him it wasn't happening. He'd understand friendly banter. No doubt flirting came to him as easily as breathing.

He raised an eyebrow. 'We'll see about that.'

'I want to be honest with you, Mauro. I'm here for the charity, because my work insisted on it, and for a week in the sun. I'll smile for the cameras and if you want to get to know each other while they're rolling then fine. But that's all. No funny business.'

He held her gaze for a second longer than was comfortable. What was he seeing? What was making him search her features like that, as if he was trying to get inside her head?

Managgia, she was driving him crazy already. He'd fixed her with his most challenging look. The one that had got impossible contracts signed, and unattainable goals achieved. And she still hadn't shown him who she was. She was carrying this front of hers like some sort of armour, and all he wanted was a glimpse at what was behind.

He'd heard the real her on the show, he was sure. The take-no-prisoners, 'I'd be a killer whale' Amber. The one whose caustic humour had hit him so hard he'd had to go off script, just to see what happened if he called her bluff.

So where was she now? Because she damn sure wasn't in this airport with him. Instead, in her place, was a woman trying to appear… *ordinary*.

Was she soft underneath? he found himself wondering. Like the silk shirt she'd worn beneath that blazer the first time he'd met her. The one that had gaped slightly between the buttons, that had skimmed gently over her generous breasts, hinting at the shape below just enough to keep him awake last night, concealing him enough to drive him crazy.

What had happened to make her so…closed? So controlled? Where had these defensive walls around her appeared from?

At least she had made it clear that she hadn't expected anything from him this week. It was why he had gone off-script and chosen her, of course. When he had been swimming competitively it had been his time in the pool that had controlled his schedule, his time, his life. Now it was time in the boardroom, trying to steer his sports marketing company from one market-leading success to another. There was no room in that life for a relationship. It simply didn't fit. If he was going to achieve everything that he wanted in this life—everything that he needed to—then he had to be focussed.

Since his university friend had driven the car they were travelling in into a tree, leaving him with a spinal injury and a brush with death that had been closer than was comfortable, he'd been determined to do more. To see more. To *be* more.

Before the accident, he'd been a naturally talented but under-committed athlete. The thought of leaving this world with just a mediocre list of achievements to his name: a bronze medal in the university swimming championship. Scraping a two-two in his Sports Marketing degree. A girlfriend he had liked a lot, but not loved. Not enough, anyway.

After the accident? It had all changed. It had to. He wanted to leave a mark on the world. So he'd watched the ParaGames from his hospital bed with an interest that had bordered on obsession. Four years to get himself fit, to be the best in the world. And he'd done it. Six gold medals over two games. And then after a day in the pool or the gym it was packing as many more achievements and successes as was humanly possible: flying lessons, professional development courses, a one-night stand with a beautiful woman. Anything new, anything remarkable, anything to make his life meaningful. To drive him further and further from the mediocrity that had almost been his epitaph.

And after he retired from swimming, he'd attacked the business world with zeal. The seeds he'd planted when he was competing started to grow, and somehow, ten years later, he had money rolling in from sponsorship deals, which he'd used to set up his own sports marketing business, his half-dozen medals hanging in his Sicilian home, and a passport that had seen almost as much action as his super-king-sized bed.

This front of Amber's was meant to keep people at a distance, he guessed. To keep herself apart, private. She must not realise how much he could see. How her hurt radiated from her like an inflamed wound; how her strength and her vulnerabilities were so tangled together he couldn't seem to see one without seeing the other.

He had thought that he was picking the least complicated option, when he had chosen Amber. That she was someone who couldn't be less interested in a relationship with him. And yet now, with this strangely fragile front she was presenting to the world, she suddenly seemed more complicated. More dangerous.

And now she was off again, without a backward glance at him, elbowing her way through the crowded shop to the till. He followed in her wake, through the path that her elbows had created between the tourists, and caught up with her.

He gripped his wheels tightly with his fingers. Because despite every well-reasoned argument he made about why he absolutely, definitely could not get involved with her, it was taking all the self-control he possessed to stop himself reaching out and brushing his fingertips over her skin. Pulling her down to sit on his lap so that he could explore today's silk blouse, tug at the ends of that prissy pussycat bow and satisfy his need to know what it hid beneath. Whether she was peaches and cream or strawberries; firm and toned or soft and yielding.

Because it didn't matter how much he wanted to know, the fact remained that trying to find out would be a very bad idea indeed. She was the walking embodiment of complicated, and he didn't need that in his life.

He pushed through the crowds after her, wondering how he had found himself chasing again. It wasn't a situation he found himself in often. He'd got used to a slightly embarrassed deference when he was with other people—he'd heard, 'Oh, no, after *you*...' so many times that it made him wince. He was so different from the youth he had once been in so many ways—the money, the medals, the chair—that he wasn't sure which of the three it was that had that effect on people. All he knew was that whichever it was it didn't have an effect on Amber. It seemed there was actually a chance that he might have a normal conversation this week. One with someone who wasn't an employee, or a fan, or trying to get into his bed or his bank account. How refreshing. How utterly tempting.

He forced the thought away as they left the shop and the crowds thinned.

'Now we have something to keep us entertained on the flight, what next?' he asked. 'More shopping? More champagne?' Keeping themselves busy seemed like the best defence against his thoughts wandering in inappropriate directions, like sliding down the neckline of her silky blouse.

She glanced at the screen in the centre of the terminal. 'They've announced the gate number. We get priority boarding, right? Might as well head straight over.'

'Sure, if you want.' What he wanted was to take her shopping for one of the teeny tiny bikinis he could see in the window of the shop opposite. What, so that he could torture himself by looking at something that he couldn't have? He'd need his self-restraint locked down before they reached his pool later, with sunshine and Prosecco in abundance.

He just hoped that she was going to be taking care of her own sunscreen. The thought of smoothing his hands over her shoulder blades, lifting her blonde hair to one side and tracing the nape of her neck with his fingers, rubbing cold lotion into hot skin… He imagined her, muscles relaxing under his touch, leaning her weight back against him as his hands skirted her sides, dipped into the hollows of her waist, found twin indentations at the base of her back. Would she object if his hands drifted lower still, if they dipped into the waistband of that tiny bikini?

'Mother—' Amber stopped and grabbed her foot, pulling it up to nearly waist level and inspecting the grubby mark across her shoe, which looked suspiciously like a tyre mark. 'Watch your wheels, Mauro!'

Damn. He'd caught her toes like a complete novice and all because he'd let his thoughts get carried away, imagining something that he could never allow to happen. She was still standing on one leg, grimacing, and gripping her toes as if she were worried they might fall off.

'I'm sorry, Amber. Here, let me see.' Before she could protest he'd wrapped an arm around her waist and pulled her down onto his lap.

Caught off guard and off balance, she fell into him without protest, her bum landing on one thigh, her injured foot propped on the other.

'Mauro! What the hell; let me up.'

His arm was still wrapped tight around her waist—even as he was doing it he knew what a bad idea it was, but he'd just run her down, and it wasn't as if he were a waif. Between him and the chair they were well capable of doing some serious damage to a little toe.

'How about we wait until the smart wears off, *cara*? Don't tell me it doesn't hurt—I can see that it does.'

'It doesn't hurt so bad that I need to be in your lap.'

'It's nothing,' he said, wishing that he could believe what he was saying. 'It doesn't mean anything. Just think of me as a convenient seat. One of the underrated benefits of using a wheelchair, in my opinion. I'm very useful to have around when there's swooning going on.'

'Swooning? I didn't swoon, you tried to cripp—'

He saw the blood drain from her face as she realised what she had been about to say and stuttered to a halt.

'I mean—I meant—I didn't—'

Oh, he would enjoy this. Finally, a crack in this Ice Queen's façade. This was the most out of her comfort zone he'd seen her since that screen had pulled back and she'd realised he hadn't taken her 'back off' bait.

He raised an eyebrow, waiting for her to speak.

'I wasn't thinking.' The words rushed out of her as she desperately tried to backtrack and swerve around the very politically incorrect word that had nearly escaped her mouth. 'I would never use that word if I was talking about…'

Flames were devouring her face and there was an earnest, beseeching look in her eyes. OK, that was probably enough.

'Relax—' he nudged her shoulder with his own '—I know that you didn't mean anything by it. It'll take a lot more than accidentally dropping the C-word into conversation to offend me.' He'd learnt pretty quickly after his accident that it was the intention behind a particular word that would offend him, rather than the word itself. In his opinion, *that* word used among friends was far less offensive than being labelled 'brave' by someone who knew nothing at all about him.

In her horror at what she had been about to say, the fight had left her body, and she now sat comfortably in his lap, leaning just ever so slightly into the arm around her waist. Maybe sitting a little too comfortably. He might have lost a lot of the sensation from his legs, but his spinal injury was incomplete—doctor-speak for the fact that his spinal cord hadn't been completely severed—and those nerves that were still attached? Boy, were they doing an awesome job right now. And his eyes? There was nothing wrong with those. Nothing wrong with his nose, either, which was drinking in the rich scent of her hair by the lungful; or his hands, which were begging for permission to take hold of that stubborn chin, angle her luscious mouth down towards his own, and take the kiss that he'd been completely unable to stop imagining from the moment that he had first seen her, however much he had tried.

Or maybe he didn't need to use his hands at all, because she was turning towards him all of her own accord. Those big hazel eyes were locked on his, until they dropped and he just knew that she was looking at his lips. He flicked a tongue out to moisten them, to tempt her into reacting to him. Her skin flushed again as she watched him, her eyes not leaving his mouth. He moved closer, a centimetre, and then another, waiting for the moment when she blinked, when she realised he was getting too close, and froze up on him. When there was nothing but a couple of millimetres between them he breathed in another lungful of that intoxicating scent and closed his eyes, desperate for the moist warmth of her lips on his.

And then the wind was knocked from his chest and they were wheeling across the floor. Someone must have barged his chair out of the way. His hands went to his wheels as her arms tightened around him.

Brakes, Mauro. He'd never been so relieved to have made such a schoolboy error. If he'd put on the brakes he wouldn't have just been barged across the terminal building. She'd still be sitting in his lap, her lips on his, rather than scrambling herself upright. He was going to have to be more careful if he wanted to keep his life exactly as he liked it, with nothing getting in the way of his ambition and his achievements. The only relationships he had space for were simple, honest flings where both parties knew what they were getting and were happy with the bargain.

A relationship with Amber would be anything

but simple. Something about the brittleness of the front she showed the world told him that she had been broken. It was as if the pieces of her didn't fit together quite right, leaving chinks to the hurt and vulnerable woman underneath.

'What the hell? Did someone just *push* you?' She spun around, looking for a fight. Nice deflection, he thought, wondering why she was so angry at herself.

'Leave it, Amber.'

There had been a time when he'd have chased anyone trying to push him around—literally or metaphorically—and shown him just how much damage a bloke with a spinal-cord injury was capable of inflicting with his fists. It just so happened that when you used a wheelchair you were at the perfect height for one or two particularly vulnerable targets. But he'd long accepted that some people would act like idiots around him. He could either let the anger consume him, as it had sometimes threatened, or he could learn to rise above it. To be the bigger man and show the world what he was capable of with his medals rather than with his fists and fury.

He glanced up at the flight information screen and realised that they had no time to pick a fight anyway. There wasn't even time to head back to the lounge and meet Ayisha and the cameraman—they'd have to hope that they would make their own way there without them.

'Come on,' he said to Amber, his resolve cracking for a second and brushing his hand against her hip. 'They're calling our flight.'

As the car swung into the driveway of the villa Amber caught her breath. The low-slung walls of the building were rendered in white, which in the late afternoon sun seemed to glow a warm orange. Three sides of the building wrapped around a central swimming pool, with expansive glazing, so every part of the house had a view of the water. Through the floor-to-ceiling windows, Amber could see straight through the building, through more windows, to the clear blue-green of the Mediterranean. She stopped as she was climbing out of the car for a moment, stalled by the beauty of Mauro's home.

Somehow, even though Ayisha had told her to expect luxury, she'd been expecting the sort of villa she and her ex, Ian, had stayed in during happier times; the sort with slightly noisy plumbing and grass growing between uneven paving stones in the garden. This—this was something else.

Imagine being able to call this your own, she thought, her mind wandering back to her bedsit in a grimy part of London. She was grateful to have a roof over her head at all, but to think that this was real life for Mauro, not a week of playing house… Their lives couldn't be more materially different. It was bad enough that he was a millionaire, successful in every aspect of his life, whereas she was just holding onto her job by a thread. They had to rub it in her face with this beautiful house as well. Not that he was going to be interested in her, with her bargain basement clothes and her grubby flat. Not that she wanted him to be.

She turned to look at Mauro.

'This is beautiful.'

'Thanks,' he said with a nonchalant shrug. 'Come on, I'll show you around.'

She wasn't sure why, but somehow she found the idea that they were staying in his house more unsettling than if the production company had hired somewhere neutral. As if it handed him a massive advantage over her. And that wasn't the only thing unsettling her. There was the memory, too, of what had happened in the airport. The way that she had sat in his lap, hypnotised by his mouth. The slight smile tugging at the corner of his lips, the way his tongue had moistened them, readying them to meet her own.

If they'd not been interrupted…

But thank God they had, and she didn't have to think about how that sentence could end.

As Mauro gave her a guided tour of the property, she was blown away by the sheer luxury of the place. The gleaming chrome of the coffee machine, the soft, supple leather of the sofas, the expansive cotton and silks on the beds. Every now and then a detail caught her eye—a handrail, a switch to lower a kitchen counter, a tile underfoot that felt particularly grippy—that made her realise all the subtle adaptations that had been made to the villa in order for it to function perfectly as Mauro's home. A million miles away from the clunky white bars and red strings she'd seen in the disabled loos at work.

'And I thought you might like this room.'

He opened the door into one of the guest suites and Amber caught her breath at the view of the ocean from the wall of windows. The water stretched green-blue as far as she could see. The view drew her in, closer to the windows until her fingertips were resting lightly on the glass. There was nothing between her and the horizon. No one but a handful of fishermen in their brightly coloured boats between her and the edge of the world. Mauro crossed the room and pressed a button on the side wall, upon which the glass doors concertinaed until the whole wall was gone and there was just a few hundred feet of terrace and sand between the bed and the ocean.

'Mauro, it's incredible.' Amber's voice caught in her throat, and she cursed herself. She didn't even understand why she was feeling so emotional. Perhaps it was the fact that she'd lost her home, that she didn't even have that West London shoebox to her name any more. Perhaps it was the knowledge that all of this had come from Mauro's many successes, when she was barely keeping a job using the one talent that she had. Maybe it was the fact that she'd spent the last eight hours on edge, desperately trying to keep her hands to herself, her libido in check, and her thoughts from wandering to Mauro.

At least he seemed to be shying away from the issue as well. Since that moment in the airport they'd both been studiously well-behaved. It all added up to exhaustion, physical and emotional.

'I was going to offer you dinner. My housekeeper will have left something in the fridge, or I can arrange something to be brought in.' He took another look at her. 'Or I can let you crash and see you at breakfast?'

She knew the relief on her face had shown when he gave her a concerned smile.

'I'll leave you to it.' He showed her how the controls for the window wall worked and let her know that he'd be in the pool if she needed anything.

Once he was gone she sat heavily on the bed, still in awe of the understated splendour of Mauro's home. If she had been unsure before about whether she wanted to succumb to Mauro's advances, this had been the wake-up call she had needed. Their homes couldn't be more different, their *lives* couldn't be more different. She absolutely would not get involved with him.

CHAPTER THREE

MAURO WOKE TO the smell of rich Italian coffee percolating through the house—Amber was up already, then. He gave a half-smile. He hadn't expected her to be awake first—had thought that she would be making the most of the holiday with a long, lazy lie-in. He had planned to be in the pool, fifty laps in, before she emerged and wanted to float on a lilo with a cocktail in hand. So she'd caught him out already. He didn't like it, the way that she kept him guessing, kept proving his assumptions wrong.

It had made him wonder what else he'd been getting wrong lately.

His bedpost certainly wasn't lacking in quantity of notches, but, now that he thought about it, there hadn't been much variety, much challenge. He'd left hospital after his accident with the single goal of achieving and seeing as much as any person could in a lifetime, and now a whole aspect of it seemed…samey. Dull.

But those meaningless flings had been exactly what he had wanted. His ex-girlfriend had made it perfectly clear that his ambitions and commitment to his sport didn't leave room for a partner or romance. He had failed at it once, and he had no interest in revisiting that disaster.

He pulled himself up in bed and transferred to his chair with a quick push of his arms. They still had a little time together before everyone else arrived. Once they'd had a quick breakfast and he'd done his laps for the day they were to meet Julia, Ayisha and the cameraman for that day's filming. The usual stuff, he supposed—by the pool, on the beach, and a 'romantic' dinner for two. And in the meantime? He still couldn't satisfy his curiosity, his need to understand more about her.

He wheeled through to the kitchen and found Amber sitting at the table, espresso cup in hand.

'Morning,' he called out to her as he came into the kitchen and headed for the coffee pot, still hot on the stove. There was something about being home in Sicily that brought his Italian blood out; if he were in England, he might start the day with a cup of tea and toast, but as soon as his feet were on Sicilian soil it was espresso or nothing.

He pulled up to the table with his coffee and reached for one of the pastries she'd piled onto a plate in the middle of the table. He expected his fingertips to meet flaky, buttery pastry, but instead they landed on impossibly soft, slender fingers as Amber reached for the *cornetto* at the same moment. He pulled away at the same instant that he registered her flinch. He couldn't help the sting of rejection at that tiny movement; whether he wanted her to be interested in him or not, that small pull away from him hurt. It was just his pride, he thought as he met her eyes, daring her to acknowledge the contact, the electric flicker that he had felt when their skin had touched.

But she backed away from the challenge, lowering her eyes and snatching her hand back.

So she really wasn't out here to play that game. Good. He decided to get them back on more neutral ground. 'All ready for your day as a reality TV star?'

She groaned, and he laughed at the look of horror on her face.

'I'm not sure I'm ever going to be ready,' she admitted. Her face had relaxed, and he could tell that she was relieved he hadn't called her out on what had just happened between them. Well, she didn't have to worry on that front. Ego had made him hold her eye just then, but that didn't mean that he had any intention of actually exploring that spark further.

'So why sign up in the first place?' he asked. She looked as if she had been regretting her decision ever since, after all.

'Sign up? I'm not sure that's how I'd describe it. It was more like...railroaded, or threatened. Definitely something that doesn't count as volunteering. And it's for charity. How could I say no? It's not like I ever thought...never mind.'

Oh, he knew exactly what she'd never thought, whether she was going to finish that sentence or not. She'd never thought she'd be here, never thought that she would be the one chosen. Well, in fairness she hadn't been. The TV company had had it all worked out—of course he'd been meant to pick contestant number two—but then with the cameras rolling and a live audience—what could they do when he picked the wrong woman? His agent had given him an earful, of course, but it had been worth it.

And what were a few booked flights and cancelled reservations when you had earned a fortune and were willing to use it to get what you wanted?

'Sorry I spoilt your masterplan. What can I say? I like a challenge.'

He instantly regretted his words, because he absolutely didn't want her getting the wrong idea. It wasn't that he wouldn't seduce her in a heartbeat if he had thought that she might be up for a fling. But it couldn't be more clear that a simple dalliance wasn't on the cards with her. There was too much hurt behind those eyes, too many defences built around her. The ghost of romance past haunting her expression.

And as much as he wanted to back away slowly, keep his distance from the big scary emotions that were clearly behind that controlled front, there was something in there calling out to him. Some vulnerability that made him want to protect her. To find out if there was anything that he could do to help.

He didn't want to think too much about why.

Perhaps, if nothing else, he could give her an ego boost. She clearly needed one. He could see it in her dropped eyes, the way she pulled her shoulders in to protect herself. Someone had given this beautiful woman cause to doubt that she looked like an absolute goddess. And as he couldn't give the person who had done that to her the hiding he no doubt deserved, then maybe he could at least get her to see what he saw, without any danger of either of them wanting to be any more involved.

'So you're not dating anyone? There's not some boyfriend hiding away somewhere while you raise money for the kiddies?'

'No.'

That wasn't a 'not right now', or a 'nobody special'. That was 'never', 'definitely not' and 'not ever' all rolled into one. He had been right: there was a world of back story behind that one word.

His voice dropped to a gentle murmur. 'Do you want to talk about it?'

What was he doing? Talking about a bad break-up ranked right up there with sticking needles in his eyes on his list of enjoyable activities. But there was something about this woman that he couldn't ignore. He couldn't brush her pain away and pretend that he hadn't seen it. If spilling her heart over her breakfast was what she needed he had a horrible feeling that he was signing up for the whole messy performance.

She took a long gulp of her coffee, and painted on something approximating a smile. 'There's nothing to tell, really. I broke up with someone a year and a half ago and have no intention of repeating my mistakes. I think maybe I'm just one of those people who are happier alone. Independent.'

Perhaps. Or perhaps not. Because as she spoke he could see the lurking shadows of grief and disappointment in her expression. The memory of someone who had let her down. Had left her feeling…less than she was.

'Or maybe you just need to—'

'Get back on the horse? Because there are plenty more fish in the sea? And someone better is just around the corner? Sorry but I've heard the clichés all before. Perhaps some people are just better suited to not…riding. Sorry, I'm better at the metaphors when I've had more coffee.'

She laughed, but it sounded hollow, thin. He had been right when he'd assumed that a quick fling would never be on the cards.

'I'm going to head out to the pool for a few laps before the cavalry turns up,' he said, trying to get them onto safer ground. 'Can I tempt you with a dip?'

For a second he thought she was going to say no, but then a smile appeared on her lips, a real one this time. 'Actually, that sounds good. I'll go get changed and meet you out there.'

The day was already warming up as he made his way out to the pool, unseasonably balmy for this time of year. He was going over his conversation with Amber again. He wanted to make her see how beautiful she was. After a decade of mutually satisfying but emotionless seductions and flings, this was new ground. He might have had a sensitive side once. It'd just been so long since he'd had any call to get in touch with it he wasn't sure that it was even still there.

He lowered himself into the pool and lay back in the water, letting it take his weight as he soaked up the warmth of the early autumn sun. His eyes drifted closed as he enjoyed the freedom to power himself around the pool, moving effortlessly in the water in a way his body didn't allow him on land. He heard her before he saw her, the flip-flop, flip-flop of her sandals on the tiles at the water's edge, the soft rustle of cotton as her towel hit the sunbed. Looking up, he saw the fluffy dressing gown she was wearing, and realised that he had been hoping for something else, something revealing, maybe. A better look at that body that she normally kept so well hidden beneath skimming silk.

She dropped the robe only at the last minute, as she slipped into the water. He had the briefest glimpse of a utilitarian one-piece in black and white, with thick straps and a racer back. Most definitely built for speed rather than decoration. Disappointed as he was, he had to admit to feeling a little pleased at finding that they had something in common.

'You're a swimmer?' he asked. Maybe he should have guessed from her strong shoulders and her toned limbs, but it seemed that his mind had been elsewhere since they met.

She shrugged, crossing her arms in front of her. 'Maybe when you're not in the pool to show me up. Given present company, let's just say I like to swim.'

'So if I were to challenge you to a race?'

'Then I would politely decline the chance to further inflate your ego by letting you whip me.'

He laughed out loud as he crossed to the side of the pool. Now there was an image he would normally enjoy.

'How about a few friendly lengths, then?'

She pulled her goggles down over her eyes. 'Fine, but no splashing.' For a moment, she paused and sniffed the air above the water. 'No chlorine?'

'It's salt water,' he told her. She *was* a swimmer, then. Any fantasies that a rebellious part of his mind might have had about a little heavy petting in the deep end were being firmly quashed.

She pushed off from the side of the pool and sliced through the water with a stroke that was perfectly decent if a little loose in places. He saw the hesitation at the end of the length and knew with an athlete's instinct that her tumble turns were not going to be the smartest part of her repertoire. He watched her for a couple more lengths, tracking the movement of her limbs as she executed each turn, looking for places to pick up a little speed, lose a little resistance. It was what had made him a champion—that ability to deconstruct every move in the pool, looking for tiny improvements, all of which added together made for six gold medals and a whole ream of world championship titles.

At the end of her fifth length she paused with her hand on the wall, and threw him a look over her shoulder, as if she had only just remembered that he was there, still watching.

She gave him a long look, and then her eyes narrowed. 'Come on, then, out with it.'

'Out with what?'

'Either you've seen something wrong with my performance here, or you're blatantly ogling me. And I've already told you that I'm not interested.'

How dared she? It was taking all his self-control *not* to watch her in anything but a professional manner, and he was pretty damn impressed with himself for managing it. He wished he *had* been ogling her if that was all the thanks that he got. The only way to prove it was to tell her exactly what she had been thinking.

'You really want my advice?'

He saw the hesitation in her eyes, and the way that her shoulders dropped forward defensively, automatically. She'd taken criticism before, and often. It was clear in the way that she smoothed her features so that her expression was carefully blank before she looked up and met his eye.

She needed him to be kind.

The knowledge struck him in his gut, and he knew without having to be told that someone, somewhere, had been beating on this woman's self-confidence until all that was left was the presence of mind to pretend that she didn't care.

'Well,' he said, choosing his words carefully as he crossed the pool to her side. 'Your basic stroke is great: you really power through the water. But if you want me to help you with your tumble turns, we can save you some time there.'

Her shoulders dropped, just a fraction, and he let out the breath he had been holding. A smile crossed her face, slowly, chased by a look of fierce determination.

'Let's do it.'

'That's it. Perfect. Amazing!'

Amber let her body go loose as she rested

her head on her arms at the side of the pool, a small smile turning up the corners of her lips. Her lungs were burning and limbs aching. She'd performed turn after turn after turn, tucking tight and exploding out until she knew—even before Mauro said a word—that she had nailed it.

She didn't care about the exhaustion. It was totally worth it. She'd struggled with those turns since she'd first taken up swimming, and if this was what it took to get them right, she'd be out here in the pool with Mauro every morning.

She'd wanted to die, at first, at the thought of stripping off in front of a world-class athlete, conscious of the wobble of her thighs. Conscious, too, that her swimming had always been the one part of her life that Ian's criticism had never been able to touch. For half an hour, every morning, she had been able to put one arm in front of the other, kick as hard as she could, shake off the tension and anxiety of living in fear of his next piece of 'advice'.

'You really got it that last time. You want to try one more?'

She shook her head, knowing that she had given the pool everything that she had. 'I'm spent for the day. Anyway Ayisha and the others are going to be here soon, aren't they? I think she said something about lunch nearby. Are they going to interview us both? Try and make us say something embarrassing about each other?'

'What could we possibly have to say? We've both been on our very best behaviour.'

Well, she wasn't sure if that was exactly true—that time when she'd sat on his lap in a public place, that didn't feel exactly like something a good girl would do. And the way that his eyes had followed her in the pool… She could tell the difference between public and personal interest, and his professionalism had slipped more than once. The heat in his expression had warmed her cheeks. When she looked up now and met his eye, what she saw there could have set the whole pool simmering.

'Well, this is cosy!'

Amber spun in the pool at the sound of Ayisha's voice, to find herself looking straight down the lens of a TV camera. She forced her smile into place and held it there until it felt as if her cheeks were cracking.

'We were just—'

Amber forced herself to keep her features neutral as Mauro draped a casual arm around her shoulders. 'Ayisha, hi,' he said. 'We were just finishing up here.'

She shrugged the arm off, as casually as she could. She knew that she needed to show a softer side on camera, but that didn't mean she had to get all up close and personal. Not yet, and definitely not when she was undressed and exposed.

'I'll see you inside.' The words came out almost as a squeak, but Amber remembered to keep her smile in place as she boosted up out of the pool, grabbing for her robe before she was fully out of the water. She couldn't help but be aware that the camera was rolling, that she had to be on her guard, protecting herself and her reputation whenever that red light was on show. 'I just want to shower the salt off and then I'll be out.'

She pulled the towelling tight around her as she walked from the pool, wondering how much the camera had caught between her leaving the meagre privacy of the water and the safety of her robe. Ian had told her often enough how out of shape she was, even with her exercising every morning, and the last thing that she wanted was her wobbly bits exposed on TV. She pulled her shoulders forward slightly, hiding the curve of her breasts from the camera, and headed as quickly as she could towards the open door of the villa.

CHAPTER FOUR

SHE WAS STILL rubbing at her hair with a towel when she came out of her bedroom. She could have lingered in there longer, but leaving Mauro with the TV crew didn't seem like the best of ideas. She knew from being in the studio with him that he was capable of being deliberately provocative, saying whatever he thought would get the biggest reaction. It was as if he was so used to his Casanova persona that he didn't think at all. Just flirted on reflex, made suggestive bedroom eyes at any woman in a fifty-metre radius. But he could be different in private, she had noticed. He was still polite, of course. There was still that heat between them when their eyes met, however much they were both trying to ignore it. But there was a distance between them as well, a barrier that he held strong when they were alone, but that seemed to disappear in public. As if he didn't mind *appearing* to be close to her, but making it very clear when they were alone that he was strictly off limits. Well, that was fine by her. It was exactly what she needed if she was going to use this show to save her career.

Mauro had pulled up to the kitchen table in his chair, and another steaming cup of coffee was sitting in front of him. Julia was sitting on the other side of the table, chin resting on her hand as they chatted.

Julia fancies him, Amber thought. Oh, she was hiding it well. The flirtatious persona Julia had oozed in the studio was nowhere to be seen now the camera was off—she was the very definition of professionalism. But the nervous touches of her hair and the frequent glances at Mauro's lips gave her away. A surge of red-hot emotion shot from Amber's belly to her jaw, and she took a deep breath, trying to identify it. Jealousy? How could she be jealous when she had no interest in Mauro? Well, as long as it didn't impact her image on the show, then Mauro and Julia could get up to whatever they wanted. Except that thought made her stomach turn; made her want to stake her claim so that the other woman would back off.

The intensity of the feeling took her breath away.

She couldn't allow this to happen. Couldn't allow that feeling, that urge, to hold any sway over how she behaved. She'd come to Sicily with only one goal—to save her career. She needed to show the British public a softer side to her character, and flirting with Mauro was the best way to do that. But the more time she spent with Mauro, the harder it got. Every time she saw his professional gaze slip and a flash of bedroom eyes instead, every time she felt the press of his skin as he straightened an ankle, turned a hand, in the pool, she was more and more sure that this wasn't just playacting. Her body wanted him, and it didn't care that her head was screaming for her to stop. To hide and protect herself. Not to let her feelings anywhere near a man who had blown through woman after woman without looking back.

'Don't worry, no camera this time,' Julia said, breaking her dangerously racing thoughts and pushing a cup of coffee towards her.

'I was just filling Mauro in on the plans for the rest of the day,' Ayisha chimed in from behind her. 'We'll head out to a restaurant from here, film you guys over lunch. Then we'll pull you out individually for some interviews. This afternoon you two will hit the beach with us in tow. Some sunbathing, some water sports, then we'll wrap it all up and you'll be on your own this evening. Sound OK?'

But her brain had got stuck on water sports, a safe avenue of thought at last. 'How will we...?'

'What, you think using a wheelchair means you can't jet-ski?' Mauro raised an eyebrow in her direction and she suspected there was more to this question than met the eye. A test, maybe. Was she going to expect limitations from his chair? Or would she, rather as he did, she suspected, see his life in terms of what he *could* achieve, rather than what he couldn't.

'To be honest I've never really thought about it before.'

There was no point lying and saying that she'd spent long hours wondering about the ability of paraplegics to participate in adventure sports. But that didn't mean that she was going to underestimate him now. 'Somehow I suspect there isn't anything that you can't do if you set your mind to it.'

He held her eye and his mouth twitched up at the corner. If that was a test, she guessed that she'd just passed. As he refused to look away, she felt the start of that smile radiate from his face to hers, as her mouth seemed to mirror his without any input from her.

'Right, we're off,' Ayisha said reluctantly, looking from one of them to the other, and the moment was gone. 'If we're not going to be filming here then we need time to set up at the restaurant. Are you absolutely sure that we can't—?'

'Certain, I'm afraid. It's just not going to work, having cameras in the house,' Mauro said. 'We'll meet you there.'

Amber's hands fidgeted as she waited for Mauro to return. What had just happened? For a moment it was as if she and Mauro had been completely on the same wavelength. As if they had shared exactly the same thought, with no conflict or tension between them. It made her nervous. Because fancying the man and pretending to flirt with him, that was something that she could handle when she knew absolutely that there would never be any chance of anything emotional developing between them. But that look had suggested something different. It had hinted at common ground, and them being connected.

The slick sound of Mauro's wheels on the tiles warned her that he was back.

'I thought you might be happier if we kept the cameras out of the house as much as possible,' he said as he picked up his coffee cup and then drained the contents.

She was touched that he'd thought of it. Who was she kidding? She was more than touched. Ian had never considered her feelings like that. Looking back, she realised he'd actually tried to make her uncomfortable, if he'd had the opportunity. He'd liked her off balance. Because that was when he'd been there for her. He'd liked to create situations that were impossible for her to tolerate, just so that he could 'rescue' her.

Now Mauro was doing the opposite, trying to smooth the distress from her life, and she didn't know how to handle it. Why? Why was he being so kind?

Could it just be the playboy at work? Was this simply a seduction technique, a ticket to an easy, grateful prize?

'I'm not a complete idiot, you know.' He turned towards her and caught her hand. 'I saw how uncomfortable you were when they all turned up. It's not fair for you to have to deal with that at home. I want you to feel comfortable here.'

She took a step backwards, snatching back her hand. Comfortable? How was she meant to feel comfortable with all this tension between them, with the memory of being so close to him that she could feel his breath on her lips, waiting for her to lean in.

How could she feel comfortable when Mauro had just told her that he saw not only her face and her body, but that he saw something deeper too? He saw what she was thinking, what she was feeling. Most dangerously of all, he saw what she was trying to hide.

They needed safer ground, something less personal, less dangerous to discuss. 'I've never been on a jet ski,' she said, hoping that talking about him would lead them away from anything too personal.

'You'll be a natural, I'm sure. The hardest part's getting the wetsuit on.'

Oh, for God's sake… A wetsuit. What more humiliation were they planning on throwing at her this week? 'If you can do it, I'm sure I can…' She stopped speaking as she realised what she was saying. 'Mauro, I didn't mean that you wouldn't be able to because… Because…'

He held her gaze for a long moment. 'Are we going to talk about the elephant in the room, or are we going to keep tripping over it?' So maybe talking about him wasn't safer ground after all.

'Elephant?'

'Why don't we assume,' Mauro said, 'that I'll take it as given that you're not going to intentionally be insulting me because I have a disability? You don't have to tiptoe—see, you can mention toes and everything—around me.'

'I'm sorry.' She shook her head as she sat beside him and poured another cup of coffee from the pot. 'I don't know why I said that. It's not like I've not met someone with a disability before. Maybe it's the cameras. They make me nervous.'

'There are no cameras on us now.'

She froze with her hand outstretched, cup of coffee halfway towards him. He had caught her gaze as he had spoken, and now he refused to drop it. Blood rushed again to her cheeks and she knew that they must be blazing red. He hadn't even touched her, and already her skin was burning for him. She managed to tear her gaze away, and glanced for a split second at his hand, resting on the table. It was only a couple of inches away. It would be nothing to set the cup down, reach for his hand and let her fingertips brush gently against his skin. But he twitched away, even as the thought crossed her mind, and she breathed a sigh of relief. It was too much. Too risky. She placed the coffee in front of him and withdrew her hand to the safety of her lap. 'I'm sorry. No more tiptoeing, I promise.' She stood suddenly from the table, and headed to the door. 'I'd better go get ready if we're meeting them there.'

'So about this elephant,' Amber said later that day.

He concentrated on the electronic controls of his beach wheelchair, rolling steadily across the sandy planks of the boardwalk as they made their way across his private beach, heading towards the building that housed his water sports equipment. The heat of the sun was fading, and the afternoon was pleasantly warm in the sheltered cove.

He'd not had a chance to talk properly to Amber since she'd so abruptly fled the kitchen after breakfast. He'd thought maybe he'd have a chance over lunch to ask what had upset her, but they had been too busy fielding questions from Julia and Ayisha. Now they finally had the opportunity to finish the conversation they had started back at the villa, but she wanted to talk about him, instead of herself.

'That journalistic instinct finally winning out over social awkwardness?' he asked with a grin that he hoped told her he didn't mind answering her questions.

'Can I ask what happened?'

'Why not?' It was refreshing, after the way that she'd been watching her words around him. 'After all, this is a date, isn't it? We're meant to be getting to know each other.' Why had he said that? This wasn't really a date. It was closer to being a business arrangement. If he were to start thinking of it as a date… Well, he just couldn't; it was as simple as that. He had no interest in starting anything with Amber Harris. Every line of her muscles screamed of past hurt and vulnerability, and he was the last person that she needed in her life.

No, this definitely wasn't a date. If it had been a date, he'd be letting himself hang back in his chair, just a little, so that he could watch the swing of her hips as her feet sank in the golden sand with every step. He'd reach out and brush her hand with his free one, savouring each spark of energy, which he just *knew* would grow with every touch of her.

If this were a date, he wouldn't be fighting the mental images that were bombarding him in the aftermath of their little coaching session in the pool this morning.

But this wasn't a date. Because she was afraid, and sad, and, oh, *so* not ready for a fling. And he was ambitious, and driven and single-minded and selfish, and—according to his ex-girlfriend—the very last person that any sane woman wanted in her life.

His chair gave out a low electric growl as it fought over the sand, but he didn't hesitate, pushing the machine forward at full speed, 'There's not a lot to know,' he told Amber as they reached the edge of the water. Amber let the waves lap at her toes, and he tried not to think too much about the fact that he'd never paddle in the ocean again. There was no point dwelling—there were so many things that he could still do. So many things that he'd achieved that he'd never dreamed of doing before his accident.

He shrugged as he continued speaking. 'I was driving home from training with a teammate. The car came off the road and hit a tree; part of the car door got wedged in my spine.'

She drew in a short breath in shock. 'Well,' she choked, 'that's one way of putting it.'

'Honestly—' She was looking out at the water, her eyes on the horizon, but suddenly he wanted her attention. All of it. If he was going to talk about the most transformative time in his life, he needed...connection. He didn't want to just throw the words out into the air and hope that they reached her. He needed to see, to know, that she understood. He caught her hand, and, though she tensed, she didn't pull away. He held on tight, not because he wanted romance, but because he wanted—no, needed—her to get this. If she couldn't understand this, then she couldn't understand *him*, and suddenly nothing seemed more important.

'No one believes me when I say this, Amber, but I'm lucky. I'm alive; I have enough money that I can get pretty much anywhere I want. I have the equipment to keep in shape and I have the sort of perspective that only comes from a near-death experience. You're not going to be one of those terrible, terrible people who tell me you'd rather have died, are you? I'm not sure I could take that. Not coming from you.'

'Not from me? Why not? What's special about me?'

What was special about her? Well, actually he had a list of what was special about her. It started with the way her skin felt as it slipped, wet, under his fingers, and went from there. But why the hell had he said that when they'd been talking about his accident? Why should it bother him any more than normal if she was one of those people who just didn't understand him, who couldn't see how much life he had left in him? He shouldn't care. He'd promised himself ten years ago that he was going to do the things he needed to in life. Anyone who wasn't OK with that had been left behind and had no one but themselves to blame.

But he couldn't bear to hear her speaking as if there were nothing remarkable about her. It made his blood boil to think that someone had let her down so badly that she could have lost sight of the truth of herself so completely. And just then he couldn't bear for her to think of herself that way. He grabbed for her other hand and pulled her in, resting both her hands on his armrests so she would have no choice but to meet his eyes.

'What's special about you? Oh, *cara*, where do you want me to start?'

With her leaning in so close, it would be nothing to reach out and caress her jaw, just a whisper of a fingertip from her chin up to behind her ear. But his hands remembered the slide of her lithe calf, her delicate ankle beneath his hands that morning, and they yearned for more. He reached for her, and his fingertips hit the soft vulnerable skin behind her knee. He let his hand rest there just for a moment as he registered the shock in her eyes. Then he raised his hands and threaded his fingertips through the salt-textured waves of her hair, until her breath was warm on his lips; until her eyes were enormous green pools just inches from his.

Just as he was closing his eyes, could practically taste the sweetness of her lips, a flash of light caught his eye and snapped him from his Amber-induced trance.

'Ayisha.' With that one word, the sensual softness disappeared from Amber's lips as they formed a concerned expression. But by the time she lifted her head, they had stretched into a sham of a smile.

A frown furrowed his brow. Why had she done that? Why fake it? It wasn't as if she'd ever made a secret of the fact that she hadn't wanted to come on this date in the first place. Perhaps she was just being polite. But…no. It was more than that. You didn't become someone else just because you were being polite. And that was what had just happened. Amber had disappeared behind the mask of this grimacing stranger.

'Looks like we're interrupting again,' Julia said with a singsong intonation that made the red light on the front of the camera behind her redundant. Of course they were filming—and the timing couldn't be worse.

'What gave us away?' Ayisha asked. He could see from the expression on her face that she was just as annoyed as he was that they'd interrupted what had looked certain to be a *very* interesting progression.

'Sunlight reflecting off the lens,' he told her, trying to regroup his thoughts, and calm his body.

'Argh, gets us every time,' Ayisha complained. 'Well, don't let us stop…uh, whatever it was we interrupted. You two feel free to pick up right where you left off.'

Tempting as that was, he had a feeling that he and Amber needed to finish this conversation—and anything else that had been about to happen—without an audience. 'Oh, we were done here,' Amber said with a strained cheerful intonation to match her smile, and again Mauro felt a flicker of anger and hurt that she was faking it like this, faking it with him.

'OK, then, if you're sure, we could actually do with cracking on a bit. We need to do some long shots first, because the light's great with you two down by the water there. So if you want to continue your…conversation we'll be way back up the beach so just ignore us. We just need to have a little look round, set up a couple of things and then we'll shout you over after we've got those shots for some interviews. All sound OK?'

His eyes narrowed as his gaze followed Julia, Ayisha and Piotr as they retreated down the beach, all the while with that little red light letting them know that they were still being watched, however far they might go. When he looked up and met her eye, it was clear that Amber had retreated from him, and it wasn't just that her hands were no longer resting on his chair but loosely at her sides. He ached to grab them again, even while he knew that it would be a terrible idea. For a brief moment there had been an intimacy between them, but he knew from the strained look that had replaced her manic fake smile that this wasn't just complicated, it had layers of obstacles that he didn't understand. Maybe he should be mad at her for lying to him, for being fake with him, but mainly he just wanted to help her. Protect her.

'That woman has terrible timing,' he said jokingly, hoping to lighten the mood.

'Oh, really?' Amber replied.

That was how she was going to play this? As if that moment had never happened? Well, good. It had worked for them so far, he supposed.

They'd both brushed off that kiss that never happened in the airport. He supposed it made sense that they'd try the same now. But they couldn't go on like that for ever; they couldn't ignore indefinitely whatever it was between them that was making him feel like this. As if he wanted to know her. To understand her. As if the more time he was spending with her, the more he wanted out of this week. More than he had ever been able to give before.

Perhaps they were going about this all wrong; if they confronted this head-on—acknowledged that there was an attraction—they'd be able to move past it.

'It's not going to work, Amber.'

She raised her eyebrows in an attempt at playing dumb.

'I know that you feel something between us.' Out of the corner of his eye, that red light still winked at him from down the beach. Damn it. She was standing away from him; in any other circumstances it would have been a comfortable distance. Close enough for conversation, not so close that he had to strain his neck looking up at her. But right this second there was nothing comfortable about it. He wanted her close if they were going to have this conversation. He wanted her hands back on his chair. Right up in his personal space with nowhere to hide. This could only work if they were both honest with one another. If there was anything left unsaid, he knew that it would just allow this atmosphere between them to fester. But he also knew that if he tried to touch her with the cameras on them, she would bolt.

So when she leaned in, her hand on his, and whispered into his ear, he could barely catch his breath with the shock of it. 'It's just attraction. Just physical, Mauro. It doesn't have to be a big deal.'

It's just—

What?

She was still uncomfortable. That much was clear in the tension showing in the muscles above her collarbones. The slightly fixed look at the corners of her mouth. She was faking this flirtation. Oh, the attraction was real enough. Her body wanted him and his was begging him to give himself to her. It seemed stupid even to try and deny that. But those casually thrown away words. They weren't her. Goddamn him, though, if he wasn't going to take advantage of this moment and try and crack through to whatever was going on underneath. Maybe he'd actually get at something close to the truth.

'Just attraction? Amber, this "just physical" thing you're talking about is testing me to breaking point. So if it's no big deal, why haven't we both stopped all this dancing around and got it out of our systems? Because we both know that there's more to it than that.'

Just saying it out loud fired a charge of electricity into the air, and it crackled between them, looking for earth, any opportunity to shoot through them and tie them together. But it was easy to throw words like that out there when you knew there was no chance of them hitting the mark. Amber might be saying all the right things, pretending that she was going to give in to attraction, but he knew that she didn't mean it. Not yet, anyway.

The more he saw of her, the more he saw of how much she kept hidden from the world, the more intrigued he was. He still wanted her to open up to him, still wanted to try and get to the bottom of the pain in those eyes, to help ease the burdens of her past. He didn't want to think too much about why. About why he couldn't just cheer her up and show her a good time and move on. Something about her spoke to him. Called out to him, and he couldn't just ignore it.

Perhaps if he opened up, spoke more about himself, perhaps then she'd start to trust him. He'd lay himself out there, and could only hope that she'd accept the challenge and reciprocate.

With a wrench in his gut he turned his chair away from her and wheeled along the water's edge. Away from that prying red light. 'You wanted to know about the chair. After the accident, they couldn't tell me a lot about what was going to happen. With all the swelling and everything it takes a while before they can really see what the extent of the injury is.'

'Did you think that you might walk again?' He glanced up and her face looked a little more relaxed. She'd jumped on the change of topic, and he guessed she was pleased that he wasn't going to call her out directly on her attempt at flirtation.

He didn't mind answering her questions. From someone else, it might have felt intrusive, but from her it was matter-of-fact. She was simply trying to understand him better rather than looking at the freak show.

'God, I hoped so. I think I spent most of those first few weeks praying to anyone who would listen that I would be able to. But my spinal cord had taken too much of a beating. So I have a little sensation in places; I've worked on what movement and strength is left so that I can manage a few paces with crutches if I need to. But mostly I feel happiest in my chair. In the right building it can get me from A to B quicker than if I was walking. The beach is a challenge, but the right equipment makes it possible, and it's worth it to get into the water and on a jet ski.'

They continued for a few metres in silence, and he guessed that she was choosing her words with care, this time. 'I'm not sure what I can say that won't sound patronising. But I find it incredible that you can think of it that way. No wonder you charge a fortune for your motivational speaking.'

'Don't start thinking I'm some sort of poster boy. I just did what I had to and thought what I had to in order to survive. It's all any of us do.'

'Not everyone,' she argued. 'Not every person who uses a wheelchair is into extreme sports.'

'No, but they do what they have to—just like everyone who doesn't use a wheelchair.'

'And you need extreme sports to get by? Let

me guess: classic case of needing to feel near death to feel alive?' Oh, she really thought she had him pinned down, didn't she?

'No, it's not that. Trust me, when you've felt as close to death as I have, you're happy keeping it at a respectful distance. Well, I am anyway. It's not the danger I love; it's the experience. It's pushing to find the limits of what my body can do, of what my mind can take in. It's finding something new in every day, to mark that day as special. To make it matter.'

They stopped again and looked out over the water. A light breeze was playing with her hair, making the sun catch all its shades of gold and silver.

'And you're telling me that has nothing to do with your accident,' she said.

'It has everything to do with the accident.' Of course it did: he wasn't a machine. It wasn't as if he could have carried on with his life without the accident having an enormous effect on him. His need to achieve, to *experience*, had infected every part of his life. His girlfriend hadn't been able to understand. She had seen the man that he had become after his accident and decided that she wasn't that interested after all.

'It changed me. What would you expect? Look: I nearly left this world as a mediocre twenty-something wasting his days on mediocre experiences. I've been pretty damn close to my highest achievement in life being winning the one hundred metres freestyle at school sports day. It's not the way I want to go. I don't need the money or the fame, though I'm not going to argue that they don't make my life a hell of a lot easier than it might be otherwise. But I need to know I'm doing something. I'm *being* someone.'

She fixed him with a shrewd look, and he felt a curl in the base of his stomach. If she was sussing him out, he had the feeling he wasn't making the good impression that he'd been aiming for.

'You like the thrill of the chase, then. The new and the unfamiliar.'

He was right, and she was getting close to the bone. Was she digging around this subject with intent? Did she want to know what he had to offer? Part of him wanted to keep his mouth shut, lie by omission, say whatever it took for her to trust him and take him to her bed. But he couldn't do that. If Amber decided that was what she wanted, then he wanted her to decide it while in possession of all of the facts.

'You think that's why I've never settled down? Well, maybe you're right. Maybe it is. But I didn't set out to be a playboy, Amber, if that's what you're getting at. I had a girlfriend. I think I loved her, actually. But that wasn't enough. It wasn't enough to compensate for the man that I became after the accident. There's not room in my life for both. I can't have this drive and ambition, and have enough time and energy left over for a relationship as well. She made that pretty clear when she packed her bags and left me. I've discovered since that when you've made it your life's mission to see everything you can, it doesn't leave a lot of time for seeing the same thing twice.'

'Or the same woman.'

He looked up at her, trying to gauge from her features whether she was judging him. 'I'm not looking for commitment, Amber. But you know that I want you.'

'I know.'

He held her gaze, challenging her with that intimacy, with the connection that he knew that they both felt.

'And if I thought for a second that a fling was on the cards then, trust me, I'd be pulling out my best moves right now. But I think we both know that that's not what you want. All I want to know is—what *do* you want? Why are you here? The truth.'

He wasn't sure why he thought that he deserved honesty from her. Really, if he thought about it, she was little more than a stranger to him. But he had shown her parts of himself that he didn't open up to just anybody. It wasn't too much, surely, to expect the same from her.

Then she broke their connection and her eyes flicked over his shoulder. He glanced behind him and saw Ayisha and Julia deep in conversation, and a winking red light on the camera that told him they were still being watched.

He could show her that she should trust him. That she wouldn't regret taking a chance and confiding in him, but he'd rather do it without an audience. Anyway, there were other ways to put a smile on a woman's face, to put some colour into her cheeks. He turned his chair and powered along the beach again, his free hand at the small of Amber's back. A couple of hundred yards later they reached the cabin where he kept his water sports equipment.

'Come on.' He tugged her hand as he drove up onto the boardwalk in front of the cabin. 'We can talk later. Now: I'm going to teach you to jet-ski.'

* * *

Amber pulled the elastic from her hair and collapsed on the sand. Adrenaline still coursed through her veins, making her heart race and every grain of sand feel like a pinprick on her skin.

'Mauro, that was… Immense. Incredible. Some other big word I can't think of right now. I don't know how to thank you.'

He had a grin plastered on his face, making his green eyes twinkle, and showing off the smile lines around his mouth.

'You don't need to thank me,' he said.

Which was a good thing, because her perverse imagination was having a few rather inspiring ideas about how she might show him her appreciation. Call her a cavewoman, but there was something about seeing him with that powerful machine between his legs, seeing him leap over waves and twist and turn in the water, that had her hotter than anyone who'd just spent an hour in the ocean had any right to feel.

Ayisha came up to meet them where they'd stopped on the sand. 'Amber, we're just going to do these interviews before we let you get changed, if that's OK with you?'

Spell broken again. Thank goodness. Because the longer this day was going on, the harder she was finding it not to sink into those green eyes of Mauro's, to remind herself of everything that she had lost the last time she had let herself be so careless, the last time that she had let her guard down. Getting involved with Mauro would be like asking for her heart to be trampled all over again. He was a playboy—he didn't even bother to deny it. Acting on this attraction would lead to nowhere but trouble. But she couldn't think about that now. She was going to have to smile and flirt her way through this interview.

She settled into the chair set up in the little gazebo on the sand, and tried to pull herself together, to make sure that she was showing exactly what she needed to make the audience find her likeable. The viewers at home—all the ones who bought her paper, read the website and held her career in their hands—needed to see that she was a warm-hearted person. Someone to be trusted, to come to for advice. Someone with something interesting and witty to say. Without readers, she had no job. And her boss had made pretty clear before she'd left that she had precious few of those readers left. She needed to make this work.

Not that it was going to be difficult to make anyone believe that she fancied Mauro. She was pretty sure that it was obvious to anyone that she was having X-rated thoughts about him. The problem was going to be keeping it likeable, and that meant keeping her memories at bay.

Broken and broke, she'd been left by the man she had thought she was going to spend her life with. Nothing could induce her to want to repeat that. No, a relationship was definitely out of the question. But it wasn't as if Mauro wanted that anyway. He'd told her he only ever had casual relationships. So even if she had wondered, in her weaker moments, whether there might be anything to chase between them, at least she could rationalise herself out of it.

'So, let's go back to that first time you met. What were your first impressions of Mauro?' Julia's question broke into her thoughts, and Amber rushed to smile, though she guessed it looked creaky. The TV presenter's excited tone told Amber—if she'd had any reason to doubt—exactly the answer she and the audience wanted to hear.

With her fake smile still fixed in place, Amber gave her what she wanted. 'Well, he's gorgeous, obviously.' She followed her words with a little laugh, which sounded tinny even to her. Relax, she ordered herself. Don't go too over the top. Julia was nodding encouragingly. 'And he knows just how gorgeous he is—never misses an opportunity to remind me of the fact.'

'Well, that sounds like Mauro, all right. So what did he do? Can you give us an example?'

'Well, this morning, for instance…' She improvised hastily, feeling the blood rushing to her cheeks. The blush would work in her favour, she thought—show that she really was human. 'He turned up to breakfast with no shirt on.'

Julia made a performance of fanning herself with her script. '*Really*, that is interesting. Not the worst start to a day, I imagine.'

'It was quite a sight,' Amber agreed. The smile this time came naturally, and she took a deep breath, forcing it into her shoulders and spine, helping them to relax. 'Unfortunately, he was just on his way to the laundry room. You can imagine my disappointment.' She let the cushions of the chair take her weight and mould round her body, finally feeling able to speak without a shake in her voice. This is all there is to it, she told herself. Just talk about how you fancy Mauro, and don't overthink the rest of it.

God, she hoped it was working. If she could

just convince Julia, and the viewers at home, that she could be warm-hearted, open to romance, perhaps they'd call off the Internet witch hunt and she could salvage her career.

'So other than the fact that he looks good without a shirt—which, let's face it, we all knew from his swimming career—how are things going? Any sparks?'

The memory of his hands on her body, his breath on her lips, of his arms around her when he pulled her onto his lap, was at the forefront of her mind. She forced herself to keep looking at Julia, when her instinct was to drop her eyes, to try and hide exactly what she was feeling. Where was the line? She needed to show a softer side of herself, but that didn't mean she had to reveal everything.

Thankfully it seemed Ayisha had seen that she had got the best out of her for now. 'I think that blush speaks for itself! That's great, thanks, Amber. That's all we need right now. I'm going to get Mauro in here and then you two are done for the day. Make sure you rest up tomorrow; you've got Mount Etna to conquer in a few days.'

CHAPTER FIVE

A WHOLE DAY passed in a blur of sun, swimming and sleep by the pool while Mauro caught up with some business on the island, and he still hadn't appeared by the time she decided to turn in for the night. But the next day she was aware of him before she was even out of bed: she awoke to the rhythmic swish-swish of a powerful swimmer in the pool. As the glass wall of her bedroom concertinaed open, the briefest hesitation in his stroke told her that he'd heard her, and he slowed to a halt at the end of the lap, before crossing to the side of the pool nearest her room with a lazy backstroke.

'Morning, sleepyhead.'

He was right—she could tell from the warmth of the tiles beneath her feet that she'd slept later than she'd planned. Must be all the sun, she reasoned. She rarely slept past six at home, was in the pool by seven and the office by eight. Judging from the hungry ache in her belly it must be nearly nine now. Long past her habitual breakfast of toast and black coffee.

'Sorry, I did wait for you, but I needed to make a start on my laps.'

'No, my fault.' She dropped to sit by the side of the pool, pulling her robe tight around her swimsuit while she let her feet play in the water. 'I can't believe I slept so late.'

Mauro placed an elbow either side of her knees. Her instinct was to pull away—but his hand brushed against her calf, and she found herself incapable of moving. Or perhaps…perhaps that was an excuse. Perhaps she wanted to stay right where she was, testing her limits, her resolve.

'I must have worn you out on the jet ski,' Mauro said with a roguish grin. 'Was one lazy day not enough? Should I have gone easy on you?'

'Never.' She smiled, but faltered when Mauro's hand dropped to her ankle, absent-mindedly caressing the delicate bones, and then found the sole of her foot with his thumb. Just…there. There was her limit. She pushed him away gently with her free foot.

'Right,' he said, raising an eyebrow. 'Where's the fun in holding back?'

She rolled her eyes at his obvious double meaning.

'So are you getting in the pool?' he asked. 'We can work on those turns some more.'

Did she want to be barely clothed, in close proximity, with him watching her every move… A dropping sensation in her tummy told her that that was a very bad idea. But he was a medal-winning athlete, offering to help her. It could be just professional interest. She looked down and met his eye, and knew instantly that there was nothing professional about what he was thinking. But she couldn't resist the lure of the cool water, the slight smell of salt in the air, the chance to stretch her limbs and loosen her joints.

She started to untie the belt of her robe but Mauro's eyes on her stopped her dead. It was bad enough that he was going to see her in her swimsuit *again*; she couldn't bear to have him watch her with that quiet intensity while she undressed.

'Erm…any chance of some privacy, Mauro?'

She tried to keep the words light, but suspected that the shake of her voice had given her away.

'Privacy? You have your suit on, don't you? There's not going to be anything I haven't seen before, you know.'

She'd expected flirtatious, playful Mauro, but instead his face was serious as he regarded her through narrow eyes. 'You didn't like that the camera caught you in your swimsuit the other day either.'

She laughed, but it sounded brittle.

'Who wants to be on telly in their underwear?'

'Well, plenty of people don't seem to mind too much, from what I've seen. But… I don't know. I just feel like there's something you're not telling me.'

'Mauro, there's a million things I haven't told you. You barely know me. Come on, I thought you were going to help me with these turns again.'

She shrugged off her robe and his questions and slipped into the water. She swam half a length under the surface, letting the water muffle the outside word. Only when her lungs were screaming for air did she finally surface, opening her eyes to see Mauro just a couple of metres ahead of her.

She took a deep breath before she turned, aware in every part of her body of Mauro waiting at the end of the lap, his eyes following the movement of every limb. She'd never felt more exposed, more vulnerable, in front of him.

Pushing away from the wall, her body was strong and straight, and she swam another couple of laps, letting the familiar rhythm of her front crawl wipe away her tension at Mauro's question. It wasn't what he'd asked—it was why he'd asked it. He must have seen something, worked out some of her past to make him wonder.

The next time she reached the end of the pool where Mauro was waiting, he reached out to her, his hand just brushing against her arm.

She pulled up, resting her arms on the side of the pool. She hadn't realised until she stopped and found herself out of breath that she'd been going at sprinting pace, swimming faster and faster to try and slow the racing of her mind.

'It's looking really good,' Mauro said, in response to her raised eyebrow. 'Even better than when we worked on it before.'

'You stopped me to tell me that?'

'Is that not OK?'

'I thought this was a training session.' That was how she'd talked herself into this, after all.

'OK…' He gave her a shrewd look. 'Let's get

to work, then. This time, I want to see those arms dead straight before you push off.'

As she neared the wall again, she glanced ahead to gauge her approach, trying to time it to the perfect arm's reach. She exhaled through her nose as she somersaulted, curling her knees into her chest. Just as she tensed her legs to power into the start of another lap, she felt a heavy pressure on her waist, immobilising her. Her eyes flew open in surprise, until her gaze rested on Mauro, holding onto the side of the pool with one arm, the other curled around her.

'It's OK—it's me,' he said, as if anyone else could have that effect on her body.

He'd misinterpreted her reaction: it wasn't panic making her suddenly breathless. It was the heat of his arm on her waist, burning into her skin where the suit was cut out at the back. It was the way he was supporting her whole body in the water, the way that her muscles had relaxed into his care, her body trusting him completely even if her mind wouldn't.

'I wanted to show you…' His voice trailed off, but she didn't move. Didn't uncoil her body, didn't seek the safety of the floor of the pool. 'You could tuck in a bit tighter, and straighten…'

His fingers brushed the inside of her arm, the oh-so-sensitive skin just above her elbow, barely a whisper of a touch. But it was enough to unravel her practised poise, until her toes were drifting down towards the glassy mosaic tiles at the bottom of the pool, her body was seeking the touch of his, and her arm—where the fine hairs were still erect from the touch of Mauro's hand—was draping itself loosely around his shoulders.

'Tighter,' Mauro said, and she wrapped both arms around him, testing how it felt to follow his commands—and her desires—without trying to rationalise.

He spun suddenly in the water, trapping her against the rough wall of the pool, his forearms braced either side of her: holding her, protecting her. When she met his eyes, it was to find that she was already half drowning in him. But where she was water, he was fire; the heat in his eyes was unmistakable, and directed solely at her.

'Amber…' Mauro began, but his voice trailed off as he broke their gaze, and he moved closer, until she couldn't resist closing her eyes in anticipation. She waited for his lips to meet hers. Instead of soft pressure of skin on skin, warm breath tickled behind her ear, and his nose nudged her hair aside. In a voice barely more than a whisper, he spoke in her ear. 'Amber, you're so beautiful.'

Instantly she stiffened. 'Don't. Don't say things like that.' She ducked under his arm, away from the spell he had cast over her.

'Like what?' Mauro asked, his expression punch drunk as he twisted around to face her.

She turned and swam, pushing her anger through her muscles until she was powering through the water.

'What's wrong?' he asked when she stopped to catch her breath.

'Nothing.' Nothing that she wanted to discuss with him at any rate. It was safer if they just forgot about this. If they pretended that that hadn't just happened. Surely he could understand. She turned and started another lap, but he was ahead of her before they were halfway across the pool. She didn't want to know how much of a head start he'd given her.

'Why?' he asked as she caught up with him.

Instead of answering, she took a deep breath and performed a tumble turn. After Mauro's coaching, she barely made a splash. But a strong hand touched at her ankle. It was for only a second, but long enough to break her rhythm. She whirled around.

'For God's sake, Mauro. Just let me swim!'

'Why are you angry that I paid you a compliment?'

'I'm not angry.'

'Then what?' he asked, genuine bewilderment showing on his face. 'Can't you at least be honest with me? I don't know what happened back there. I don't even know what I wanted to happen. But I know that I hurt you, somehow, and I want to know what I did so that I don't do it again. I'm not looking to cause you pain, Amber.'

She sighed, shaking her head. 'I'm not angry that you complimented me, Mauro. I'm angry that you lied to me.'

'When? When did I lie?' he asked.

'You called me beautiful. And I know that that's not me. So don't do it. *Please.* Don't flirt just because you think that you should. Or because you can't help it. It makes me feel crappy, and it's not going to get you anywhere.'

'I'm sorry,' he said, with a shrug of his shoulders as he leaned back against the side of the pool, but the apology was just as much a reflex as the compliment had been. 'I didn't mean anything by it.'

'And that's the point, isn't it? It didn't matter

who you were saying it to. It could have been anyone. I bet you've used that line a dozen times before, haven't you?'

'Amber, I think you're being—'

'I'm sorry, Mauro, I need to get showered.'

She boosted out of the pool and walked away, knowing that she was running because she was scared, because she was disappointed in him and in herself. And knowing that she was being unfair by walking out before they could finish their conversation.

By the time Mauro came into the house from the pool, she was showered, caffeinated, and had regained some of her composure.

'I'm sorry,' she said, as he wheeled into the living space where she was sitting with an espresso and the English newspapers.

He shrugged. 'No need to apologise. But, you know, I've given it some thought,' he said. 'And I honestly think you're a very beautiful woman.'

'Well, OK…' Amber said with a small smile. 'As long as you've thought about it.'

* * *

'Oh, my goodness. You look like a...like a goddess,' Mauro said, when she emerged from the bathroom later that afternoon. Had he learned nothing from their conversation? There *was* something Grecian about the dress that she'd chosen for their tour of the winery, and the formal dinner tonight. Pleated silk swept down from an empire line almost to the floor, and a cleverly cut neckline balanced out her swimmer's shoulders. She'd assessed the result in the mirror before she had left the room. Acceptable, yes. Maybe even attractive, which—given the cost of the dress and the cosmetics, all courtesy of Ayisha—was the very least she could have hoped for.

But a *goddess*?

'Don't,' she warned.

They had walked on eggshells that morning after their argument in the pool, and she didn't want to spoil the entente that they were delicately balancing by rehashing it.

'I thought about it before I said it, I swear.'

She shook her head as they walked out of the villa and towards the waiting car. 'Please—I don't want an argument. I just want you to cut the bull,' she said as she slid into the car beside him and pulled the door shut, lowering her voice, though she wasn't sure if the driver could understand English. 'I know that this whole week is a weird, fake scenario. We keep trying to pretend that nothing is happening, but I'm not sure how successful we're being. And just when I think that we're starting to understand each other you go and spoil it by spinning all this rubbish about how beautiful you think I am.'

'Why is it rubbish?' he asked. 'Why am I not allowed to think it's true? I'm not playing games, Amber. I'm not telling you you're beautiful because I want something, or because I think you want something. I'm just trying to be honest.'

She rubbed her forehead with the palm of her hand, squeezing her eyes tight. 'But I know I'm not beautiful, Mauro, so every time you say that to me, it's like a shot of iced water down my back.'

'Oh, you *know* you're not beautiful, therefore my opinion isn't valid.' His voice was irritatingly calm as the driver eased the car around a series of curves in the road. 'I'm sorry, Amber, but it doesn't work like that. I'm afraid I get to decide for myself whether I think you're beautiful, and I do.'

'But I'm *not*.' Her voice broke as the tears that had been threatening all day finally came through. 'If you think I am it's because I've just spent an hour applying every lotion and cosmetic that Ayisha could find in Palermo when she realised I didn't have any of my own. This isn't some sort of false modesty. I scrub up all right, that's what Ian used to say to me. I can look half-decent if I put enough time and effort in. But we both know I'm not beautiful, so just cut it out.'

'Ian.' He was quiet for a long, thoughtful minute. 'Your ex?'

Stupid—she hadn't even meant to mention him. The last thing she wanted was to dissect her disaster of a relationship with Mauro, but from the determined look on his face she guessed that he had other ideas.

'He never told you you're beautiful?'

She rested her elbow on the car door, and let her head rest against her hand, losing the energy to be angry. 'Please just leave it. I don't want to talk about him.'

'Fine, we won't talk about him. We'll talk about you, and how you've got to the ripe old age of whatever you are without being able to take a compliment. This Ian, what else did he say?'

She turned to look out of the window, at a sky that was just turning pink. 'I'm not going to talk about it, Mauro, so we can just drop this.'

'So it wasn't what he said, was it? It was what he did. What was it? Did he cheat?'

At that, another tear escaped the corner of her eye as she fought a losing battle with herself.

'Yes, he cheated.' She turned back to him and fixed him with a stare. He met her gaze, and she read pity there. She didn't want him to feel sorry for her, but if he insisted on the whole sordid story, then fine. He could have it. Maybe that would be enough to put an end to his flirtation. To the temptation she was finding harder and harder to resist. 'Is that what you want to hear? He cheated and he left me, and he cleared out our bank accounts and sold my house from under me before he went. It wasn't enough to break my heart. He had to take my home and practically everything that I owned as well. And that is why I'm not in the least interested in a relationship, Mauro. I've taken just about as much heartbreak as a person can, and I'm not stupid enough to get involved with someone else, especially someone who is as proud of you to love women and then leave them.'

'Whoa, a relationship? Involved? Who mentioned involved?'

'The flirting, Mauro. The compliments. The attention. I know you're just trying to get me into bed.'

He stayed silent as they pulled through a pair of magnificent gates and wound up the road towards a castle of warm yellow stone. Silent while the car stopped in front of a magnificent wooden door. Silent until they spotted their hostess waiting for them in a stone archway.

Mauro looked across at her, his face hard and unreadable. 'She'll wait.' His tone said, *We will finish this conversation,* as clearly as if he'd spoken the words out loud. 'I have *not* been trying to get you into bed. That's the very last thing I want, actually.' His words felt like a slap to the face, and she knew that the hurt must have shown in her expression. 'No, not because… You're beautiful, Amber. And sexy, and yes, a goddess. I'm not going to take that back. I mean it. But that doesn't mean I think we should be *involved.* I don't have space in my life for a relationship; you don't want something casual. It would never work. But that doesn't mean you shouldn't believe me when I tell you how goddamn desirable you are.'

He said it with such sincerity and passion that she couldn't help one corner of her mouth turning up in a half-smile.

'That's better,' he said, swiping at her tear with his thumb and reaching for her hand. 'I'm sorry if my compliments upset you. I honestly didn't mean them to. I'll try harder to stop, if they make you uncomfortable. We can be friendly, can't we? We have our week-long first date, with a national audience along as chaperones; we smile pretty for the cameras come December, and then we get back to real life. Every now and then we'll think back to the completely strange week that we had here. You meet Mr Right, settle down and have a dozen beautiful children; I'll continue to have my fun and grow old disgracefully.'

'I'll think about it,' she said. And then, because she couldn't help herself, she leaned forward and brushed the gentlest, briefest of kisses on Mauro's cheek.

Late in the evening, after they'd feasted on the local foods and sampled plenty of Castello Vigneto's wines, Amber took another sip of the rich, deep *vino rosso* that she was sampling and let her eyes drift closed so that she could concentrate on the sheer joy of it. Dinner had been magnificent, the vineyard both beautiful and impressive, and the fruits of their host's labours was like nectar.

And the help of a little Dutch courage, or Sicilian courage she supposed, was very, very welcome. Because she strongly suspected that she still owed Mauro an apology.

She looked longingly at the wine left in the bottle, and, for just a minute, could imagine the delicious, empty oblivion it would bring if she downed the lot. But her problems would still be there when she sobered up. She was staying in his house, after all—and somehow she didn't think that a monster headache would help their situation. She rubbed at her temples, hoping for a quick fix for the tightness behind her eyes. Nope. Nothing but an apology was going to ease it.

Mauro had disappeared with Fabrizia, their hostess, ten minutes ago. Apparently she had a painting that she thought he might be interested in buying, and Amber had wandered away to sit with her thoughts and her wine as they'd negotiated in rapid-fire Italian that she had found impossible to follow.

She crossed the room to go in search of them, but she drew up short in the shadow of the doorway at the sound of Fabrizia's voice, no longer the rattle of a negotiator, but a seductive drawl that was recognisable in any language. Amber peered out of the doorway and saw Fabrizia leaning close to Mauro, one hand resting on the arm of his chair. A shiver passed through her at the sight of that hand, of her leaning forward into Mauro's personal space, making her intentions clear, however subtly.

She held her breath, a sharp pain in her chest preventing her from calling out. Memories crashed back: finding those photos on Ian's phone. The sultry tones on his voicemail. Promising things that made Amber sick to think about. The memory of that day battered through her with full force and she started shaking.

How could she get out of here? How would she get back to the villa without them realising that she had seen them? Perhaps he wouldn't even miss her—it looked as if his plans for the evening had just got a whole lot more interesting. She shrank back into the room, but couldn't drag her eyes from the scene in front of her. But as she watched, Mauro took Fabrizia's hand from his chair, and, with his other hand on her upper arm, gently pushed her away. Fabrizia smiled, a little chagrined.

'If you change your mind…' she added in English.

For my benefit? Amber wondered. Does she know I'm listening? Does Mauro? Was that why he turned down what must have been a very tempting offer?

Why? Why would he deny himself another notch on his bed post? He'd been honest enough with her about what he wanted in his romantic life.

She watched as he rubbed both hands over his face and looked up to the ceiling for a second. On her tiptoes, she retreated back into the drawing room, not wanting him to know just yet that she'd seen that little interlude. Not until she tried to work out what it meant. She poured herself another glass of wine and was taking a sip when she heard Mauro approaching behind her. 'Are we OK?' he asked, his features showing his trepidation. 'I know we've not had a chance to talk about earlier, in the car. I didn't mean to upset you.'

'And I didn't mean to fly off the handle. I am sorry.'

'You sure you don't want to talk about it?'

Her gut reaction was a screeching no. But she'd just seen him turn down easy, meaningless sex. And she wanted to know why. She didn't want to tell him that she'd seen. Didn't want to show her hand just yet.

'I'm sorry I overreacted. I suppose I'm not used to compliments. It made me suspicious.'

His brow furrowed as he frowned. 'You know, I'm starting to think I might like to meet this ex of yours. There's one or two things I'd like to say to him.'

No compliments for him, she assumed.

'I'd count myself lucky not to have met him. I wish I could turn back the clock.'

He reached for her hand. 'That bad, huh. No happy memories?'

'I used to have some,' she remembered, letting her hand rest in Mauro's, enjoying the slow-growing warmth of the touch of skin on skin. 'Some of the things we did were amazing. The places we visited… I wish I could still remember them fondly. But what came after—what he did. What he'd been doing all along, actually. It tainted them, made everything we'd ever done… It made me suspicious of how I remembered it. There had been another woman most of the time we'd been together. When I first found out about her I wondered why he'd stayed with me at all. If he wanted her then why not just be with her? When I found out that he cleared the bank accounts and forged my signature to transfer the house to his name, I had my reason. Why leave with nothing when you can play the long game and make some money out of it?'

'Surely the police—'

'Have done everything they can, given that I have no proof. And it isn't quite enough, apparently. My solicitor pushed things as much as he could, but he doesn't come free, there's no real evidence, and funds…'

'Ran out.'

She nodded then hung her head, trying to hide the tears threatening her eyes. Mauro reached for her hand and she let him take it in his own. Now the whole sorry story was out there, the fight had gone out of her.

'I saw you just now, with Fabrizia.'

He raised an eyebrow.

'Yes?'

'I would have understood, you know. If you wanted to take her home. It looked like a difficult offer to refuse.'

He dropped her hand as if it were suddenly hot.

'Don't you dare, Amber.'

'What? I would have understood.'

Understood, yes. Been happy about it? No. In fact, she'd have been sick with jealousy.

His voice was hard and expression stern. 'You're trying to make me him, Amber, but I'm not. I might be many things, and lover of women is well up there. But I do not—ever—

cheat. I never lie—I have always been completely honest with you. I am not your ex, and I would never, ever treat you that way. Let's get that straight right now.'

She lifted her hands in exasperation. He wasn't getting it. And it wasn't as if it would be cheating when they weren't even together. When they'd both already said that they didn't want to be together. 'I didn't mean that, Mauro. I wasn't comparing you to him. This is different. I mean, it's not like this is real—'

'Enough, Amber. I don't want to hear any more.' Mauro reversed away from the sofa, putting himself out of reach. She was about to speak again, but he held up his hand to stop her. 'This might not be a real date, but that doesn't mean that you're not here at all, that I'll treat you like you're nothing.'

CHAPTER SIX

'BUT YOU COULD HAVE...with Fabrizia...'

'Yes, I could have. But I didn't want to. I want to be here with you.'

He didn't want a relationship. For ten years now he had been certain that his lifestyle wasn't compatible with that sort of commitment. But after less than a week with Amber, he was questioning that decision. He had meant what he said—he didn't want to get involved. But he wasn't sure how he was meant to walk away from her either. He was fascinated by Amber in a way he hadn't experienced before.

He wheeled nearer to her again, leaned closer still until there was no escaping his scrutiny. He wasn't going to let her get away with hiding from him. 'The way that we got here, that might have been a set-up, but that doesn't change the fact that I'm enjoying getting to know you. Why do you find that so hard to believe?'

He could see the indecision in her face. See her trying to rationalise their way out of this in the way he was trying so hard to avoid. Enough. He had to make her understand.

He knew that she wanted him: it showed in the quickness of her breath, the flush of her cheeks and the flicker of her tongue to moisten her lips. What she wanted wasn't in doubt. Whether she could trust him, trust herself, to take it was another question.

He took her hands and pulled himself closer, until his chair was butting up against the overstuffed upholstery. She didn't believe him when he told her that she was beautiful—maybe she would believe him if he showed her instead. One kiss. He could give her one kiss without it leading to more.

He shifted from his chair onto the sofa, wanting—needing—to be closer to her. He would have to be, if this was going to work. He cupped one cheek with his hand, and bit back a groan as she turned into his palm, hiding her face from him. The light from the candles set around the room caught at her face, dancing golden warmth across the tops of her cheekbones, highlighting the delicate point of her chin, and—like a beacon—the plump dip above her top lip, the very top of her cupid's bow. He wished she'd look up at him, but her eyes were fixed on the patterned upholstery.

He touched her other cheek with his fingertips and gently tilted her face up. She finally flicked her gaze up to him, but darted it away just as quickly. He ached to kiss her, but didn't just want to do this; he wanted her to know why.

'Amber,' he started, but she placed a finger across his mouth, silencing him. He still held her face in his hands, and she leaned forwards, until her nose nudged at his, and he could rest his forehead against her brow. For a moment, he couldn't breathe. Amber caught at her lip with her teeth before she let out a long sigh, closed her eyes and leaned in. She bumped her mouth against his, and for that fraction of a second it was as if every nerve in his body ended in his lips. Her mouth was soft and full, the lower lip just a little plumper than the top as it slipped too briefly against his. Electric shivers of desire burned through every place that their skin touched, and he yearned for her, for more. He knew that he had to be patient; he trusted that if he gave her space she would come to him.

Just as he was about to lose his mind with aching anticipation, she whispered his name. When he opened his eyes, all he could see was Amber. Her lashes, thick and long and a deep charcoal black, cast feathery shadows on her cheekbones, hiding her feelings from his view.

She still didn't know.

If she truly knew how beautiful she was, she wouldn't avert her gaze like this. She would be a beacon, bold and fearless, demanding everything that was her right.

He nudged at her chin, and smiled as she finally raised her eyes, defiance in her features. He couldn't tell her what he thought of her, so he would show her with the heat in his eyes as he looked at her; the way that he let his fingertips dance over the lines of her face, tracing where the candlelight caught at her features, light and shadow. He rubbed his thumb gently across her bottom lip, making sure that she knew that that spot, just there, had been keeping him awake at night.

Just as he was about to lose reason and reach for her again, her hands threaded into his hair and she pulled his lips to hers.

Fire burned through him again, great walls of flame spreading through his veins as she opened her mouth to him, tasting and testing and demanding. With the taste of her, any pretence of self-control was lost. He pulled her closer and her legs across him, folds of bronze silk moving with her, sliding under his hands. With the curve of her bottom nestled in beside him, and the whole sweep of her thigh just waiting for his hands, he finally lost the power of thought. She tasted of espresso and vanilla, of rich red wine and Marsala, and as she shifted on his lap he turned her to press her tight against his chest. And then she was on top of him, a knee either side of his hips and her long, beautiful, perfect spine beneath his hands.

She murmured his name again as he broke their kiss, but it was lost in a sigh as he pressed his lips to her throat. He opened his eyes and lean shoulders filled his vision; he noticed for the first time the light spattering of freckles, coaxed out by the Sicilian sun. They were like stars dotted across the sky, he thought as he brushed his lips against one galaxy, and then another. He followed a constellation down to her collarbones, and breathed in the smell of her rosemary shampoo as his kisses found her neck.

He didn't care that this was a terrible idea, didn't care that it couldn't go anywhere. All he could care about was this, right now: the slide of silk beneath his palms as he ran his hands over calves, thighs, and cupped firm buttocks. The sound of her gasp as his palms explored higher: the smooth sweep of her waist and then back to the warm bare skin of her shoulder.

As he shifted round, tried to fall back against the arm of the couch and pull her with him, he remembered where they were, remembered that Fabrizia could walk in at any moment and find them. He closed his eyes again, but it didn't work. Real life had found them, and the *clip-clip-clip* of stiletto heels on a stone floor broke into his consciousness. Fabrizia, nearby.

Amber must have heard it at the same moment he did, because she sat up, breathing fast, and clutching at the neckline of her dress. They both looked across at the door in the same moment, and Amber jumped up.

When Fabrizia walked in, Amber still had her back to the doorway, and Mauro could see her rearranging her expression as she was brushing imaginary creases from her dress.

As she gathered her bag and wrap, and gave their thanks for a wonderful evening, Mauro realised that Amber couldn't hide the golden glow, like an aura around her that he had helped to light, and she was keeping burning.

They said goodnight to Fabrizia, and he wondered whether Amber would call out the woman who had tried to seduce her date. But in the end, she had settled on a classily subtle smile and a kiss on each cheek, as the memory of their kiss so clearly radiated from her expression.

Why had she done it?

She had known from the day that she had met Mauro that he would bring nothing but trouble, and now here was where she paid the price.

With the clarity of the morning after, she knew that a kiss like that *had* to come at a price. For those few minutes last night, she'd forgotten who she was. She had been the imperious goddess that Mauro told her he saw, oozing confidence and sex appeal. But it had been safer there, where they had known, deep down, that an interruption must come sooner or later. Alone in the villa, they had no such safety net.

'Mauro…' she had started to say when they'd returned.

'Do we need to talk about this?' he'd asked.

'I think we do. It's not that that wasn't…nice.'

'Nice?'

The expression on his face told her exactly what he thought of that descriptor and she grinned shyly.

'We both know what it was,' he said.

'OK…' she conceded. 'I know what it was, and nice doesn't even start to… But it was a one-off.' She nodded her head emphatically, but wasn't sure who she was trying to convince more. 'Considering that we have both said that getting involved isn't what we want, let's just say that it was a mistake. A very enjoyable one,' she added at the sight of his raised eyebrow, 'but we should forget that it happened. And keep it just between ourselves, of course. I don't want anyone to know, Mauro.'

Last night that had seemed like the only sensible thing to do. This morning, she had to ask herself, was that really what she wanted? She had come here with the intention of showing a softer side of herself on camera, maybe flirting a little to get the job done. But now that there was something real between her and Mauro, every instinct that she had was telling her to hide it. To bury it. To shove those feelings somewhere she didn't have to think about them. Somewhere they couldn't hurt her. She knew that it didn't make sense. But there was no room in what she had with Mauro for examination. For expectations. If anyone else were to find out what had happened, if they were to start asking questions, then she was going to have to think about them. She was going to have to think about how she *felt* about what had happened, and she just couldn't.

That kiss had been nothing more than enjoying Mauro's body—part of the weird fantasy life that the TV company had constructed for her this week. That, and their killer chemistry. He had told her that he thought she was beautiful, and just for a few minutes she'd chosen to believe him, to see how that might feel. Now those moments of madness were over, she just had to bury the memory somewhere deep, where it couldn't hurt her.

And she had to do it fast, because in less than an hour she was going to be on camera, talking about how their date was going. If she got it wrong, her job could be at stake. Ayisha kept telling her to be herself—but she was herself when she was writing, and look where that had got her. As good as unemployed, the last time that she looked. The whole point of her being here was to be someone else, someone that the public liked more than they liked her.

If she was herself on screen today, then what would the public see? What questions would she have to answer? What parts of herself would she have to expose?

In a steaming hot shower, she pushed her memories away, deep into a distant, hidden corner of her brain. Somewhere she hoped they could stay safely during their interview. Good practice, she told herself. For when they left this place and her time with Mauro was just a fond, distant memory. Not something that would affect her in real life.

She dressed in a light silky beach dress, burying the memory of Mauro's lips where her collarbones were exposed. Tying the shoulder ties a little tighter to cover the cleavage that Mauro had touched so reverently. The plan was for them to have a lazy day on the private beach and in the grounds of the villa. A luxurious picnic had been packed, along with several bottles of ice-cold Prosecco.

She had said little to Mauro since they'd discussed their kiss—it had hardly seemed necessary. They'd said everything they'd needed to already, after all. They both knew that they didn't want to be involved. They both knew that the kiss had been a mistake.

When she breezed out of the bathroom with her carefully practised air of nonchalance, it was to find Mauro wearing a killer smile and another crisp white shirt, waiting for her in the kitchen. He whistled through his teeth as she approached, and Amber fought hard to keep the reaction of her body down to a brief stutter of her breathing and the lifting of the hairs at the back of her neck. Not bad, she thought. She might carry this off yet.

'We're going to be late,' she said.

'Everything OK?' Mauro asked, and she could hear the concern in his voice. 'Is there something I've missed?'

'Nothing, nothing. I'm fine, Mauro. I just don't want to keep them all waiting. The sooner we start, the sooner it's over with.'

He followed her out of the door, but she could still feel his eyes on her. Not the sensual caress of his gaze from the night before, but a harder, more calculating stare. She shrugged off the feeling of unease. She was imagining things.

They walked down to the beach and found the crew waiting for them at a gazebo, where a loveseat with white linen covers was being set up for the interview. Gauzy white curtains fluttered on three sides of the structure, protecting the seat from the warmth of the afternoon sun.

'Mauro, Amber, great timing,' Ayisha greeted them. 'The light's perfect so we need to be shooting in about ten minutes. Get yourselves on the sofa, we'll throw some make-up on you both and then get started.'

'Both of us?' Amber asked, feeling the foundations of her protective walls take a little pressure. The last thing she wanted to do was share her true feelings about Mauro with the world. That would mean acknowledging her feelings, acknowledging that, much as she tried to avoid it, something stronger than simple physical attraction was developing, something that had the power to hurt her if she dared to acknowledge it.

She would only be able to keep herself safe from hurt if she could block last night from her mind, but how was she meant to do that if she had Mauro sitting next to her? Close enough to touch, to kiss, to smell. To remind her of everything that they'd shared while she pretended to all the world as if none of it had ever happened.

But she didn't see what choice she had. By the time that she had opened her mouth to protest, Ayisha was already deep in conversation with Piotr, and Mauro was moving over to the loveseat. Amber sat herself primly at the other end, shifting further and further away, until the rattan arm of the chair was biting into her waist.

'Relax, *cara*, I won't bite, you know,' he said in a low voice that reminded her of last night. Reminded her that she hadn't minded all that much when his teeth had trapped the flesh of her shoulder, just hard enough to make her gasp.

It took all her self-control to keep her face

neutral as she looked over at the TV crew, praying that there were no microphones on them that she couldn't see.

'Don't, Mauro.'

'Don't what?'

Did he really not know what he was doing to her? Or was this an act—was he trying to lead the conversation back to that kiss?

'I just need to relax and get this over with, and I can't do that if I'm thinking about you biting, or thinking about yesterday, or about…you at all. So just don't, please.'

I can't do this if I'm thinking about you. Why had she said that? She wasn't thinking about him. She'd spent every minute today studiously *not* thinking about him. And now she'd gone and said that and he was going to think that it was this whole big thing, and then they'd have to have a conversation, *another* conversation, about how much neither of them wanted a relationship, and then she'd have to die of awkwardness about the whole thing as they went through the motions of the last few days of the holiday.

'I'm sorry,' Mauro said, and Amber gave a small smile at the sincerity in his voice. 'This interview's going to be fine. Just be yourself.' She rolled her eyes with a huff, and he frowned.

'What?' she asked.

'Don't do that. Don't put yourself down like that.'

'I didn't—'

'You did. You rolled your eyes when I told you to be yourself.'

'Well, yeah. It's not the greatest advice. Turns out, when I'm myself, pretty much everyone hates me. Or hates my work, at least. No, I need to try being someone else: I'm just not sure who yet.'

The line reappeared between his eyes, the one that told her that he wasn't happy, but before she had a chance to ask why, Ayisha had appeared in front of them with her tablet computer, demanding their attention.

She smiled, or tried to. The corners of her mouth turned up, but she knew it hadn't come anywhere close to reaching her eyes.

'Come on,' Amber said. 'Game faces on—let's get this over with.'

She pulled her mouth into even more of a grimace, but he couldn't return her attempt at a smile. Game face? What game exactly was she playing? She'd told him already that she had been railroaded into this by her boss at work, but that didn't explain why she couldn't just be herself on camera. It didn't explain why he could see the protective defences being erected around her as clearly as if they had been barbed wire. She had been herself on the first show, he was sure of that. So what had changed? This forced smile, this fakery—it wasn't *her*.

But if a game face was what it took for her to relax, to take a deep breath and shuffle closer to him on the seat… He'd play along—for now.

Before he could say any more, the make-up artist was drenching them both in powder, complaining about the shine from the sun lotion that Amber had used to protect her skin. As soon as it had been banished, Julia was in front of them, they were miked up, and a steady red light was warning him that they were both being watched.

'So then, you two,' Julia began. 'Here we are more than halfway through your date. Can you tell us how it's going? Do we need to book a church for the wedding or separate flights home?'

Mauro forced himself to keep his eyes on Julia, and not to share a conspiratorial look with Amber, however tempting it might be. He waited for Amber to speak, but no words came. He stepped in, trying to cover their awkwardness with breezy self-assurance.

'Ah, Julia. You can't expect us to tell you all our secrets, can you? A man's allowed a little honour, after all.'

'So coy, Mauro,' Julia said with her trademark

tinkling laugh. 'That's not what we're used to from you. Surely you've got a little gossip for me.'

'Well, I think you can safely say we don't need the separate flights. Can't we, Amber?'

He glanced across at her and knew instantly it was a mistake. She looked up at him at the same time, and when their eyes met he knew that heat flashed between them. That they saw not each other, sitting formally awkward here, but memories of heat and passion, of eyes locked together in intense desire, fingertips and lips exploring and tasting. And then that, all that, was gone, and in its place Amber's eyes flashed horror and then fear.

'Of course there's nothing going on,' she said to Julia, her voice just a little too loud to be considered natural.

He knew that they needed to cover this. Whatever her motivation for this act she was putting on, he guessed that it must be important to her. Well, he'd always heard a believable lie was as close to the truth as possible. The best way to cover up what had happened between them was to act his usual, flirtatious self. As if this were nothing. 'Not for want of trying on my part,' Mauro said, stretching an arm around the back of the seat with a mock yawn. 'I've tried my hardest to seduce this beautiful woman, Julia, but so far she's resisting my charms.'

'Oh, really, I imagine that's taking quite some personal discipline. Are you finding it as difficult as Mauro seems to think you should, Amber?'

Come on, play along, Amber. He willed her to do it, to pick up his thread and weave the story that would keep their cover. They could still save this. He brushed her shoulder with his knuckles, knowing that the move was make or break. The physical contact could tip her over the edge; make her so mad that she spilled their secret. But, as he had hoped, instead she leaned back against his arm, and turned to give Julia a blazing smile.

'A man with his reputation? I don't think he deserves an easy time of it, do you? He should have to work for at least one of his conquests, I think.'

Julia laughed and leaned in close, resting her hand on Amber's in a show of intimacy. 'And are you planning—' she waggled her eyebrows like a pantomime dame '—on being conquered?'

'Oh, you can't expect a girl to answer that,' Amber answered in a sultry purr. 'You have to allow us some secrets, Julia.'

Mauro bit back his surprise. A few minutes ago he had been sure she was about to lose it at the thought of giving themselves away, and now here she was flirting like a pro. Why had she changed the rules? Where was the sharp, witty, spiky woman that he was growing to—?

Growing to what? He stopped himself short with that thought.

Not love. Never that.

Love was standing still. *Love* was saying

goodbye to ambition and achievement—not to mention saying goodbye to every other woman he might ever meet. *Love* was losing sight of all the pleasures and experiences that he might have if he kept looking for the next woman, the next adventure. His lifestyle wasn't compatible with love, and he wasn't prepared to give it up. He wasn't prepared to fail another relationship, another woman. Letting Louise down had been bad enough.

He conducted the rest of the interview on autopilot. Aware somewhere in the animal part of his brain that Amber hadn't let go of his hand. She was gesticulating with the other, telling some anecdote from their wine tasting. If the story had really happened, he didn't remember it. She was playing a part, playing up to the camera and to Julia. It hadn't bothered him the first time that he had seen her do it. But he knew her better now. Knew what she was hiding, knew that she was being this other person because she didn't think that the real her was good enough. And she was using him to do it. Using him to pretend that Amber Harris wasn't the goddess that he knew her to be.

He didn't like it.

Because it wasn't just her own life she was rewriting. His memories, his experiences were being whitewashed too. Last night, with its heated touches, and soft silk and moist lips, if she was making out as if it never happened, then he was missing out too. She was leaving his life with a giant hole where once there had been sweet seduction.

And all because her confidence had been so battered that she couldn't face up to what they felt for each other.

He wanted the real Amber here with him. He wanted her *really* answering questions about what they were doing. About how she felt about him. About where this was going to go. He shouldn't have to ask her that. This thing was meant to go wherever he wanted it to—which was precisely nowhere. Since when did he need The Talk? He had to pull himself together.

They wrapped up the show, and he held his temper and his tongue until they were on the boardwalk up to the villa and safely out of view of the camera. 'What happened back there? Who was that on the seat with me? Because I didn't recognise her one bit.'

That was it. Deflect attention from his own feelings. Perhaps if he could make this all about her then maybe he wouldn't have to admit how conflicted the last hour had left him.

She sighed and shrugged her shoulders. 'The way you looked at me, Mauro. We might as well have just told everyone what happened last night.'

'I get why you want to keep it quiet,' he said, 'but it wasn't that bad.'

'It was worse.' She wrapped her arms around her waist as she walked beside him. 'I just hope that it doesn't make the final cut on the show.'

Some chance—the whole show only existed

to capture moments like that, and he didn't think that this being a celeb version would get them an easy ride. 'You know if it was that obvious they'll definitely use it.'

'I can only hope that they don't.'

He let out a sigh of exasperation.

'Would it be so bad? It was just a kiss.'

For a moment her face fell, and he knew exactly why. If she had described what had happened between them last night as 'just a kiss', he would have been fuming. He knew, deep down, that it was so much more than just the meeting of two mouths. 'If everyone knew that something really had happened, rather than just a bit of flirting?' Her face showed him that for her, yes—it really would be so bad. 'To have everyone watching to see what happens to us. To have the story grow, be manipulated. To be asked what's happened between us when we've both decided to move on and leave it behind us? It'd be awful.'

'So why all the flirtation, Amber?' The words

burst out of him in frustration. 'It doesn't make any sense. You don't want people to know that we've kissed, but you want everyone to know that we're thinking about it? What, are you worried people will think we've slept together?'

'It's nothing to do with sex.' Her voice was irritatingly calm, as if she could reason her way through every question about what was happening between them. Make sense of it all when he was struggling. 'Why do you have to bring everything down to that level?'

'Bring it down? Based on our kiss last night I think the sex would be pretty damn transcendent.'

Transcendent? *Managgia*, he was in real trouble. It was bad enough that he was thinking that way, never mind saying it out loud.

'*Transcendent?* Mauro, what's going on? Are you OK?'

He stopped in front of her, blocking the way so that she would have no choice but to look down at him. 'You know what? No. I thought we were being adults about this. I thought we were being honest. I told you what I want from you, from this. From us. But I don't think you were honest with me. And you certainly weren't honest in that interview. If you're going to use me like that then you could at least have the decency to tell me what's really going on.'

She dropped down to sit on a bench beside him.

'Who says there's anything going on?'

'I do. There's something you're not telling me and I want to know what it is. Why were you acting like that?' He pulled at her hand and lifted her chin with his thumb so that she couldn't escape his gaze. So that she couldn't hide what she was really thinking.

'It's what the show wants,' she said. 'I was just playing along.'

She was lying; it showed in her eyes.

'And since when have you cared about what the show wants? You didn't care when you were talking about killer whales, did you?'

'Yes, but that was before—'

She stopped herself with tightly pursed lips, stood up, and made to walk away. He still had hold of her hand though, and he kept it tight in his.

'Before what? Finish your sentence. Please,' he added, when he saw the stubborn set of her chin.

'That's not what I was going to say.'

'Bull. This thing only works if we're honest with each other. I thought I'd been pretty clear that I don't mess women around, and I don't like to be messed around in return.' That was the reason for the ache in his chest and the churning of his stomach. He just didn't like to be made a fool of. He would feel like this with anyone who was being dishonest with him. It didn't mean that he…that he loved her. It couldn't. 'Either we're honest with each other, or we end this now.'

'Please, Mauro—' she reached for his hand '—it really doesn't have to be a big deal.' She threw her free hand up in a show of nonchalance. He didn't buy it for a second. Finally, they were getting to the bottom of what was going on. 'It's just…after we filmed the first show? My editor told me a few home truths. Apparently my work isn't going down well with the readership. I need to…lighten up. Show a softer side. If I don't? Well, the bosses are looking for places to trim headcount, and I'm going to be easy pickings.'

The churning in his stomach stopped, and for a moment it felt empty. Less than empty. As if a gaping hole had left him incomplete. 'And you're using me to do it. But it doesn't make sense. If you want everyone to know you have a softer side, then why all the secrecy? Just tell them we're having a torrid affair. The tabloids will love it.'

'Because if we tell people what's going on, then how are we meant to move on after that, Mauro? When we leave here I just need to be able to move on and forget it. And if the whole world sees what happened, I'm not sure how we do that. Just because I'm showing a softer side doesn't mean I have to share my whole life. I just need people to *think* that we could be… whatever. I don't want people to actually know. It's nothing to do with real life. It's just a show.'

'But don't I get a say? Don't I get a voice in this? You weren't alone last night, you know. They're not just your memories you're playing with. You told me that Ian tainted your memories, when you found out what he had been up to. Well, what do you think it does to mine when you deny it ever happened?'

She had dropped back onto the bench beside him and her elbows were resting on her knees. Worry lines marked her face, and suddenly he could see the pressure that she had been under, the genuine fear that she might lose her job.

'I'm sorry,' she said. 'I didn't think. I didn't realise that it would hurt you. All this, it all happened before that kiss, and we had both said that nothing was going to happen between us, and then last night *did* happen, and I didn't have time to come up with another plan. I didn't realise that it would hurt your feelings if I just went along with what I knew Ayisha wanted.'

He was hurt. Hurt that she had saved smiles and laughter for the cameras and not for him. That she felt closer when she was pretending to like him than when they were really alone together. He wanted to bring some light to her eyes, wanted to make her laugh, make her smile. But even after everything that they had shared last night, she still had to fake it.

'Let's just go,' he said. They needed to forget this, forget the kiss, change the subject. Because if they didn't it was going to gnaw away at him in a way that he didn't understand. 'Let's sit by the pool and drink Prosecco and watch the stars come out.'

'So do you have a thing about stargazing?' Amber asked as she sat back beside Mauro on the double sun lounger. 'Or is this just an excuse to get me on my back?'

He looked at her in surprise, but saw from the grin on her face that she was joking.

'I'll have you know,' he said, reaching for one of the glasses of Prosecco on the table beside him and passing it to her as she settled beside him, 'that I am quite the astronomer. See there—that one…that's the plough.'

'That's Orion,' Amber said with a laugh, lying back beside him. 'But nice try.'

'OK, you rumbled me. I like to just lie here and think. There's nothing like a clear sky to help you clear your mind.'

'I'll drink to that.' She took a sip of Prosecco and pulled a soft wool throw over them both. 'What are you thinking about?' she asked. 'Is it your ex?'

Where had she got that idea? He'd not thought about her for years, not properly, anyway. Well, not until this week. For some reason, memories of their relationship had been clearer in his mind than they had been for an age. Especially those last months when it had become clear to them both that what they had wasn't working, and wasn't going to last.

'Maybe it was.' It made as much sense that it was memories of him and Louise that were clouding his mind as anything else.

'How did it end between you two?'

Trust Amber not to ask if he wanted to talk about it, just dive in there with the hardest question. Well, he couldn't exactly expect an easy ride from a journalist. Amber wouldn't be Amber if she weren't constantly challenging him. He'd berated her earlier for not being honest with him, so he had no choice now but to tell her the truth—she deserved that. Maybe it would help them both, he thought. Show her why he was so sure that he wasn't meant to be in a long-term relationship, make her see that there was no point trying to think that anything might happen between them. She didn't have to worry about keeping her distance from him: his lifestyle would make it easy for them.

'Louise ended it. She said that there wasn't space in my new life for her, and that it was best we just went our separate ways.'

'Was she right?' Amber shifted onto her side, propping her head on her hand as she looked at him intensely.

'She was. By the time she called it a day, I had been away for five weeks, travelling and training. I hadn't had time to see her. It made sense to end it.'

'Five weeks without the chance to meet up? It is quite a long time.'

'Exactly. She was right.'

'But other couples go longer,' she added with a brief shrug of her shoulder.

He remained quiet.

'Or they find time to fit in an hour together. Or they talk over Skype, or they…' Her voice trailed off. 'I'm not… I'm not saying that you weren't right to end it. But—'

'But what?'

'Your colleagues, your other competitors. Do they manage to have relationships?'

'Some of them.'

'And don't you wonder how they make it work?'

Of course he had. But he had always just assumed that they were different. That they had something that he didn't. And he told Amber so.

'You think they're less committed? They don't train as hard? They don't take their work as seriously?'

'No, of course not.'

'Then what could be different?' she asked, and he had no reply. 'Perhaps…' She hesitated. 'Perhaps the relationship is different. Perhaps they make it work because they can't imagine life if they *didn't* make it work.'

He considered it. When Louise had broken it off with him, could he have fought harder? Could they have done something different?

'What is she up to now?' Amber asked. 'Let

me guess, she's a stay-at-home mum. Husband works in finance. Holiday snaps from the Caribbean and skiing in the Alps shared on Facebook every year.'

He raised an eyebrow.

'If you hadn't had your accident, do you think you would have stayed together? Would it have been you in those photos?'

He tried to think back to what he and Louise had planned together before his accident; what they had said they wanted. Was that what she was aiming for all along? The cute kids and the holidays and the house in the suburbs? Because that was never going to be him. Whether he had been injured or not, he knew that he couldn't have been happy in that life. 'So…what? You're saying that me and Louise were doomed from the start?'

'Of course not. I'm saying that perhaps your relationship was perfect for that time in your life. But as you grew older, maybe you would have grown apart anyway. Perhaps your accident sped that up, but, even before then, could you see yourselves growing old together?'

He stayed silent for a few long moments. Was she right? Had he been wrong all this time, and it wasn't him that had sabotaged the relationship? Perhaps they just hadn't been meant to be. And where did that leave him with Amber? If his lifestyle wasn't stopping them, then what was?

CHAPTER SEVEN

BY THE TIME she emerged from her bedroom the next morning, dressed in combat trousers and T-shirt, ready for their hike on Mount Etna, she'd made a decision. Last night, looking at the stars with Mauro, had been foolish.

She'd let her curiosity get the better of her, asking about Mauro's ex, and it had steered them into very dangerous waters. Today, she had to be sensible. She had to put that kiss behind them and forget any crazy ideas she had had about Mauro and her. So today was all about Operation Forget the Kiss. She hadn't meant to make Mauro change his mind about relationships, but show him that his assumptions about his last girlfriend might have been off the mark. Somehow, after Mauro's thoughtful silences, she suspected that she needed to be more careful than ever.

But she had her defences firmly in place, so she'd spend her last couple of days enjoying the island and not fantasising about her and Mauro.

'Morning,' she said, flicking him a wave on her way to the coffee maker already steaming on the stove. 'Sleep well?'

'Like a baby,' Mauro answered. 'Were you up early? I thought I might see you in the pool.'

'I got in a quick session before you were awake. I didn't want to presume on any more free coaching.' And she hadn't trusted herself to be in the pool with him. That was a key part of the plan—be sensible. There was no reason why two adults couldn't get through two days together without locking lips. Even two adults who found each other attractive. And were living together. And had already kissed once anyway. They just had to make a resolve and stick to it.

He didn't comment further on the fact that

she hadn't waited for him, and she took that to mean that he understood why she had done it.

'So I never asked,' Amber said. There she went again, being sensible. If they strayed into risky topics, like, say, whether they should be in the pool together, then she should change the subject as quickly as possible. 'This hike that we're heading out on. How's that going to work? Not in that chair, surely?'

'I've got a hand cycle,' Mauro replied, smiling and looking at her closely. 'It's been a while since I've taken it out so I'm looking forward to it.' His words sounded stilted, and she wondered if he was thrown off course by her attitude this morning. He shouldn't be. It was what they had talked about yesterday. But for some reason, it seemed Mauro still wasn't happy about it. Well, it was nothing. He'd get over it, she was sure. There'd be someone else along to entertain him and distract him soon enough. He wouldn't be lonely for long.

'Are you looking forward to the walk?' he asked. 'You've brought boots and stuff?'

She'd not worn her walking boots since a weekend to the Lake District that had involved a lot more wine than walking, but she hoped that the hours that she put in keeping fit in the pool would mean that she'd make it to the top of the mountain unscathed.

She nodded as she took a bite of her pastry—she really could get used to Italian breakfasts. 'Yep, Ayisha let me know that I'd need walking gear. It's been a while but I'll be fine. Have you been before? To Etna, I mean.'

He nodded. 'Yeah, I've been going ever since I was a kid. It's like nowhere else on the planet, Amber. It's so raw up there. Exposed. There's nowhere to hide.'

A shiver ran down her spine and she wondered whether that had been meant as a challenge.

She wasn't sure how to respond. So this was what it was like when you tried to pretend the most mind-blowing kiss of your life had never happened.

Etna loomed on the horizon as they drove through the heart of the island, the fields all around them scorched by a summer of fierce sunshine. Silence filled the car as they ate up the miles, the mountain growing ever larger before them. Amber kept her eyes on the landscape, too afraid of what it would lead to if she brought her attention closer to home. She had tried to strike up conversation, they both had, but with the black hole in the middle of their small talk all attempts had fizzled into nothing.

She jumped nearly out of her skin when Mauro's hand brushed against hers when they both reached for the bottle of water in the holder between them.

'Whoa. What's wrong?'

'Nothing,' Amber said quickly. 'You do remember, Mauro, that I still don't want Ayisha or the cameras to see what happened between us?'

How was this so hard? All they had to do was

pretend that they had never kissed; pretend that she didn't know the scent of his skin and the taste of his lips. When they had talked about it before, it had seemed so simple. The kiss was meant to get their lust out of their system; once she had acknowledged the attraction, had answered the million questions that her brain had had about what it would be like to kiss Mauro, it should have been enough. She should have been able to laugh and joke with him, without their mutual attraction hanging over them.

But the memories of those few moments in the Castello Vigneto still wouldn't leave her be. It had seemed so simple to say that they were just going to pretend that it had never happened; two days later, she still couldn't do it. She stared out of the window again, making the most of this time they had alone. As soon as they reached the base camp, the TV crew would catch up with them and they'd have to get back to faking it.

She shook her head as she looked out of the

window, contemplating the ruins her career—not to mention her heart—would be in if today didn't go well. She was worse off than when she had arrived. At least at the beginning she'd had nothing to hide from the cameras.

She glanced over at him as the car started to climb, and his jaw was set firm, his eyes fixed on the road ahead. The gleam of white on his knuckles gave away his tension and she felt a stab of unease at this hint that he was finding it as hard as she was to pretend that nothing had happened. They had to get through the next couple of days, and then they had to walk away from each other. Anything else would only lead to one or both of them getting hurt, and neither of them wanted that.

They were both going to have to get their game faces on if they were going to get through today. She needed it to go well, and for all that to happen she needed Mauro's co-operation.

'Is everything OK?' she asked.

'Of course,' he replied with a smile that didn't reach his eyes. 'Why wouldn't it be?'

Well, that was one way of assuring that she wouldn't say it out loud.

'No reason. You just seem a bit quiet, that's all. So it's not…' She didn't want to be the one to bring it up again, out into the open where they couldn't ignore it any longer. But she could feel the tension between them, could feel that their grand plan to pretend that it had never happened wasn't going to hold water. And she didn't want it there on the screen, where it might come back to bite her.

'It's nothing. Honestly.' He took his eyes off the road for a moment to turn and smile at her. 'Just concentrating on the road.' As his gaze returned to the windscreen she followed it with her own. Just as well he wasn't letting himself be distracted. The road was unlike any she'd travelled on before, with one hairpin bend after another as they climbed higher and higher up the mountain.

Mauro was driving them up to the Rifugio Sapienza, the start of the *funivia*—the cable car—where there was a collection of shops and restaurants, halfway up the south slope of Etna. It would be their base camp for the day. From there they would hike up to the next checkpoint, where the *funivia* finished, and then go on to the craters at the summit. From what she knew of Mauro, they wouldn't be taking any shortcuts.

As they climbed they passed villages that had been brushed at the edges by fingers of lava. The rivers of rock were black against the vegetation, a record of decades and centuries of rebellion by Mother Nature against the ingress of human habitation upon her territory.

Wide expanses of scrubland stopped dead as they reached the corpse of another river of fire. And then the balance shifted. No longer was the lava eating into the vegetation, but it had taken over completely, and there was nothing but rock to see on all sides.

'It's awesome,' Amber said, her gaze fixed on the changing landscape.

Mauro raised an eyebrow.

'No, seriously,' she went on. 'As in, I'm full of awe. The lava—it must have just destroyed everything in its path. Can you imagine sitting in your house in the village, and looking up and seeing that coming towards you?'

He nodded, but didn't speak. Yet more proof that, however they might try, there was no banishing the awkward. But if they could just keep it on hiatus until the cameras had finished shooting for the day that would be enough.

They continued up the side of the mountain, switchback after switchback, and by the time that Mauro's four-by-four pulled up at base camp, the landscape was positively lunar. Hillocks of coarse black rock were all around them, big enough to hide the summit of the mountain from view.

Rifugio Sapienza was more touristy than she had been expecting. Chalets housed gift shops, hiking equipment stores and restaurants, and tourists milled around, dressed in various states of propriety, from full climbing gear, with walking poles and backpacks as big as she was, to tourists who had come in coaches from the beach resorts, dressed in jeans and white plimsolls, and looking decidedly concerned about the potential of lava dust to cause serious harm to both.

Mauro stopped the car and looked over at her. 'You ready for this?' he asked.

'Which?' Amber laughed. 'The hike or the cameras.' He gave her an understanding smile, and as she looked over at him their eyes met and she felt that familiar spark, the familiar pull towards him. If she had thought that the not knowing, the wondering what that connection meant, was bad, having the answers was far worse. A couple of days ago she would have wondered what it would feel like if he pulled her across the centre console and into his lap. Today, knowing the answer to this question, it made the reach for the door handle almost impossible.

'So…' Mauro's gaze was locked on her eyes, refusing to let her go. 'It's still as we discussed yesterday? We pretend that—'

'Nothing happened,' Amber said, urgently. 'Exactly. Just like we said.'

Fumbling for the door handle while she still couldn't look away from Mauro, she all but fell out of the car. Well, it might not be the most dignified exit, but it got the job done. Got her out of danger, out of proximity with those soulful green eyes, with all the memories and promise that they held.

As she leaned back against the car she heard the click of the boot opening and the mechanical whirr of a motor. It was Mauro getting his bike out, she guessed. The one with the rugged tread on the tyre and the hand pedals. He'd trekked up Etna plenty of times, he'd told her, both before his accident and after, so he shouldn't have any problems dealing with the terrain here.

Shame—a flat tyre calling the whole thing off could be just what today needed.

As Mauro rounded the corner of the car, Ayisha stepped out from the restaurant and started asking Mauro about his cycle.

'And you're sure that you don't need a guide?' she asked. 'Because we've got a guy on standby and it'll be no trouble at all to have him accompany you, just in case you run into any problems.' She shifted awkwardly for a moment. 'Uh, so to speak, you know.' Amber waited for the laugh from Mauro that usually smoothed over this type of awkwardness, but it didn't come. And when she looked at him, those lines across his forehead were deeper than ever.

'We'll be fine.' His tone clearly brooked no argument.

'OK, no guide, that's not a problem, Mauro. It'll be just you guys, and me and Piotr will follow behind with our guide. Julia will be waiting back here for us. We'll do a couple of really quick interviews before we send you off, and then we'll try and keep our distance as much as possible. You'll both have mikes and sports cameras on, so we can hang back a bit without missing anything.'

She looked from Mauro to Amber, and Amber knew that she had picked up on the tension between them. How was she going to play it in the interviews? Amber wondered. Would she try and help them paper over the cracks so that they could get a fairy-tale ending, or as near as possible, for their Christmas TV special—or would she go for the fireworks? Push them and play them off against each other to get the dynamite material that Amber knew they could deliver. God, she hoped it would be the first one, because she and Mauro had been managing—just about—to keep smiles on their faces and the elephant out of the room this morning, but she suspected that it wouldn't take much for their awkwardness to spill over into something more dramatic. She shut her eyes against the sun and leaned back against the car. God, she just wanted this to be over. She wanted to be home. To start forgetting.

CHAPTER EIGHT

'IF YOU TWO are ready, we'll wait for you in the restaurant—the camera's all set up in there. I'd say take your time, but our guide just let us know that they're expecting the visibility to be bad later. Something about the clouds coming down. Long and short of it is that we need to get cracking if you're going to make it up there safely.'

'No problem. We'll meet you there in a minute,' Mauro said. The car journey had been a special kind of torture: he had been in that enclosed space, filled with the scent of sea salt and rosemary from Amber's hair, but completely unable to reach out and touch her. Screw the mountain roads. He would have pulled over into any layby that they'd passed if he'd thought that he could wind his fingers through her blonde waves and drag her close. If he'd thought for a second that that would have been a good idea.

If only she hadn't made everything so much more complicated by asking about his relationship with Louise. If he'd been able to go on believing that another commitment just wasn't possible, then he wouldn't be second-guessing himself and his decisions. He'd just have to get through it. Stick with it for two more days and then she would be going back to London and he wouldn't have to spend all his energy resisting her any more.

'Mauro,' Amber said, walking towards him, 'why do I have the feeling this isn't going to go well?'

He turned his lips up in a smile that he hoped was reassuring. 'It's going to be fine. You've got nothing to worry about.' But his words did nothing to smooth the lines on her forehead.

When they sat down in the restaurant, Amber painted on a fake grin, and he knew that she was going to play nice for the cameras. As the interview went on she smiled and flirted, and hinted at some of the fun that they'd had together, all the while steering clear of anything that might be considered the truth. He could feel his muscles growing tighter and his pulse starting to pick up. With every lie, the truth felt further away. The magic of that night at the vineyard was diluted, until, one lie soon, it would be as if it never happened. It would be taken from him. And it was her fault that he was feeling like this—if she'd not asked about Louise, made him reconsider everything that he'd thought about the place for relationships in his life, he'd have been able to walk away from her the same way he had from every other woman for the past ten years. He was almost sure of it.

It felt like a betrayal.

He managed to hold his tongue the whole time the camera was rolling, smiling in the appropriate places, albeit with a fair amount of subtle prompting from Julia. But the whole while, he just wished that they could talk, properly. That she didn't have to worry about protecting herself, because he would never hurt her. That maybe, if they were both brave enough, they could stop denying what was going on between them and take a chance on making a relationship work.

As soon as he heard the words, 'That's a wrap, guys,'—or maybe he just imagined them—his hands were on his pedals, powering himself out of the restaurant and out onto the surface of the volcano, leaving the whole team following in his wake.

'Mauro!'

Amber called him from the door of the restaurant, but he was too riled. They were meant to be acting as if that that kiss had never happened, and if she made him speak to her now there was no way he could do that.

He could hear rapid footsteps behind him as she picked up her pace to catch him up, but he didn't break his rhythm on the pedals. Powering himself forward, grateful for every minute he'd spent in the pool and in the gym keeping his arms and his upper body in shape.

'Mauro, would you wait up?'

But there was no need, because she'd already caught him up. Goddamn this gravel and the slow going.

'What did I do?'

He glanced at her waist, where she still wore the battery pack for her microphone.

'Nothing,' he said as levelly as he could. 'You heard Ayisha. The visibility's going to be bad later. We need to get going, that's all.'

Amber glanced over her shoulder. He followed her gaze and saw that Piotr had caught them up. Hell. Were they going to have no privacy at all today? All this, the interviews, the camera trailing them, the microphone still clipped to Amber's shirt, it all served to show him what a farce all this was. How fake the whole week and everything in it.

How much of the kiss with Amber had been

real? Perhaps she had been faking with him as well. Except he knew that couldn't be true. There had been a connection and a bond between them that was impossible for him to have imagined. And if that hadn't been real, then there would be no reason for things to be awkward—and they definitely were awkward.

But enough was enough now. He'd smiled through the interviews. He'd provided the villa and the resources and the activities. He'd even kissed her, for God's sake. What more did they all want from him? He just wanted to get on, get up this mountain, and then get on with forgetting that he'd ever met her.

Amber glanced again at the camera, and then studied his face for a few long moments. Her expression hardened, and something twisted in his guts as he realised that he had hurt her. And it didn't matter that she had hurt him first. He had promised her that he wouldn't and now he had broken that promise. He reached for her hand, and pulled her gently towards him. From the corner of his eye he could see that Piotr and Ayisha had suddenly pulled off their headphones and found some very interesting buttons to press on their equipment and were showily paying no attention at all to the two of them.

'I'm sorry,' he told her. 'Let's just forget it and go have fun. I've been waiting to show you this all week. Does that sound OK?'

She nodded, and he let go of the breath that he'd been holding.

'OK, then.' He indicated a path. 'We need to head that way. We'd better make it a fast walk if we're going to make it up there on schedule.'

He looked up at the sky, and let the sun warm his face. It was much cooler up here, at about eighteen hundred metres, and would only get colder the higher they climbed. It was a beautiful day, though. There were just a few clouds in the sky at the moment, a clear bright white against the rich blue of the sky. With the black of the lava all around, the contrast was striking. They headed away from the cable-car terminal and towards one of the paths up the mountain, along with the other rucksack-carrying, walking-shoe-wearing climbers.

His hand cycle drew a few curious glances, and they stopped a couple of times to chat to the other walkers. They trod on for an hour or so, until he realised that Amber was struggling. She'd said that she had done some walking before, but he knew that the altitude could make even an easy stroll difficult if you weren't used to it. Her face was flushed, but she didn't seem out of breath.

He tried to interpret the expression on her face. Her eyes were fixed forwards, deliberately not looking at him as they made their way higher and higher. When he glanced over his shoulder he couldn't see Ayisha—true to her word they must have been hanging back a way behind them. They were both still wearing microphones, though, so any feeling of privacy was just an illusion.

'So what do you think?' he asked eventually,

not sure how long they could keep walking without making any conversation at all.

'About what?'

He laughed, despite himself. 'Uh, about the volcano?'

He could already feel the cool of the altitude biting into his fingers. Amber had pulled on another layer since they had left the cable-car station, and the clouds were thickening above them. The other hikers had gone on ahead, what with four working limbs, and without the encumbrance of an all-terrain cycle, they seemed to be making better time than him. He glanced at the compass app on his phone, just to make sure he was still on top of their navigation and was pleased to see they were dead on course.

'Are we on track?' Amber asked, and he nodded.

'Just keep heading uphill,' he said with a smile.

They walked on, but the clouds on the horizon were starting to concern him. And the day that had started in bright sunshine was rapidly turning darker. Another couple of hundred metres passed without either of them saying a word, and he could tell from the sound of Amber's rapid breaths that she was starting to find the terrain hard going.

'Do we need to stop?'

He hadn't meant for the words to sound interrogative, but they had, he realised too late.

'I'm fine,' she bit out.

'Really,' he softened his voice. 'It's no problem if you need to take a break. I could do with a breather too.'

She snorted and he shrugged his shoulders. OK, so he didn't need to stop, but that didn't mean that he minded if it was what she needed.

'OK, then, how about if I said I'd like to stop and admire the view?'

It wasn't a lie: the view really was worth stopping for. They'd long ago left behind any signs of life; the few straggling plants that had valiantly fought for survival further down the mountain were nowhere in evidence here. But the contrast between the barren rock, the bright blue sky on one side, and the wall of white cloud on the other was unlike anything he had ever seen anywhere else on the planet. He stopped when they reached the top of the hillock they were climbing, and looked around him to get his bearings. He knew from experience that mountains could be deceptive, with one false summit following another, and when he looked around him he realised that this hike might not be as simple as he'd planned. This wasn't the summit, but he couldn't see the higher peak either. The wall of white was in front of them now, as the clouds rolled down.

He turned and looked back, and could still see the path. They could turn around and head straight back. But it was a long way down, and there was no guaranteeing that the clouds wouldn't catch up and overtake them long before they reached Rifugio Sapienza. The *funivia* terminal wasn't far—the safest thing to do would be to just keep going. And yet when he looked for the path, he just couldn't see it. They'd have to rely on the compass, the map and his memory of this trail.

'Mauro…' Amber's voice was full of trepidation. 'Please tell me you know where we're going.'

He turned to look at her and saw genuine concern in her face. Cracking a smile for the first time since they'd escaped the cameras, he told her that everything was fine. 'It's no more than half an hour from here. We'll have to trust the compass and the map, but we'll be fine.'

The tension lifted from her face, but a crease appeared between her eyebrows as they both heard the shout from behind them.

'Aiuto! Sono caduto!'

They both whipped around at the sound of the shout, but could see nothing behind them except for a wall of white.

'Che succede?' Mauro called back. *'Serve aiuto?'*

All they heard in response was a groan of pain.

Amber looked down at Mauro. 'What did you say? What's happening?'

'I'm not sure. Someone shouted for help, it sounded like he said he'd fallen, but I don't know more than that.'

'We have to go back,' Amber said.

'It might not be safe.' But another loud groan from the injured man decided for them. 'He's probably on the trail,' Mauro said. 'And he can't be that far behind or we wouldn't hear him.'

'What about the crew? Won't they have caught up with him?'

'It depends whether they turned back. I couldn't see them behind us last time I looked, and I don't know how far behind they were. But I think we have to assume that if he's shouting there's no one else there to help him.'

Amber turned on the spot, taking in the blank whiteness on all sides, before setting her face in an expression of resolve. 'Well, then. Let's get going.'

'Still no signal,' Mauro said, checking his phone as they were making their way back down the path. 'Normally I'd say one of us should go on ahead to get help, but with the visibility like this we need to stick together. At least until we find him and know what we're dealing with.'

They retraced their steps along the trail, the shouts of the injured man getting louder and more desperate as they grew close, and as he came into view it was obvious why.

The man was sitting on the ground, cradling his arm, which was bent at an ugly angle. His face was a ghostly white, bordering on grey, and his forehead was clammy with sweat. Amber dropped to her knees beside him, and murmured soothing words as she pulled an emergency blanket out of her daypack.

'It's OK,' she told him. 'We're here, and we'll get you some help. You're going to be fine.' His expression didn't change from that of shocked terror. She brushed the hair from his forehead as she sat beside him, and he flinched away from her touch.

'Can you tell me your name?' she asked gently as she shook out the blanket. 'Do you understand English? Mauro, can you translate?'

'No…need,' the man replied, shivering. 'Enzo. My name is Enzo.'

'OK, Enzo,' she carried on, in the tones one would use with a spooked horse. 'You're looking a bit chilly, a bit cold. I'm just going to wrap this around you to keep you warm. Is that OK?'

'Amber,' Mauro whispered behind her. 'Did you see his arm? We need to support it in a sling if he'll let us.'

'Mm hmm,' she said, in the same soothing tone. She appreciated his help, but she didn't need it. She could see exactly what Enzo needed, and how to help him. 'Not just now, Mauro.'

'Here we go then, Enzo.' She wrapped the blanket around him as gently as she could, keeping her hands well away from the nasty-looking kink in the bones of his left arm. 'All done,' she said. 'You're doing really well. You've got nothing to worry about. Me and Mauro are going to take care of you until Mountain Rescue arrives, and everything's going to be fine, OK?' She laid a gentle hand on his shoulder. 'OK?'

Waiting until he met her gaze, she smiled, and then turned back to her bag. 'Now then, something to warm you up.' She pulled out the flask of coffee that they had packed back at base camp and poured a cup. Holding it up to Enzo's lips, she encouraged him to take a couple of sips. 'That's it,' she said with another smile. 'You're doing great.'

Finally, she turned to Mauro, who was still behind her.

'What?' she asked when she saw him smiling.

'Nothing,' he said. 'Just…that was pretty amazing. That's all.'

She went to dismiss him with a wave of her hand, but then stopped herself. 'Thanks. But that was the easy part. We need to decide what to do next. What do you think—do we sit and wait?'

'I'm not sure that we can,' Mauro said. 'Did you see the colour of his hand? It looked to me like his circulation was compromised. The forecast had this fog sticking around until nightfall. There's not a good time for someone to find us, so I think we're going to have to get ourselves found instead. Do you think he can move?'

'Not like this.' She turned her back to the injured man and dropped her voice to a whisper. 'You saw how much pain he was in when I was just wrapping that blanket around him. You're right about needing to get that arm in a sling, but he's not going to like it. Are you sure that there's no other way?'

'Our other option is to wait till morning. What do you think?'

'Too cold,' she said immediately. 'And he's in too much pain. We have to move.'

'Agreed.'

She turned to Enzo, wondering how much he

had heard, but, from the glazed expression on his face, his distress and panic were going to be as much of a hindrance as his physical injuries.

'OK, Enzo. We have a plan to get us all to safety, but we're going to have to move. Do you understand?' She glanced up at Mauro to translate, but it wasn't necessary.

'No, not moving,' Enzo said with a shake of his head and a panicked expression. 'Hurts.'

'A sling,' Amber said. 'If we can strap his arm tight and immobilise it, it should keep the pain to a minimum. Is there one in the first-aid kit?'

'No, but we can make one from a spare shirt, if he'll let you.'

She nodded thoughtfully. 'He's going to have to trust me. OK, Enzo. I know you're scared, but we really need to get ourselves somewhere warm and safe. It's not far. Mauro knows exactly where we're going, but we need to go soon, before it starts to get dark.'

'My arm…'

'We're going to make you a sling, and make

sure your arm won't hurt while we move. Can you do that for me?' she asked, brushing the hair off his forehead again and turning his face up to her. 'Can you trust me? We're going to do this together.'

She pulled a spare T-shirt out of her pack and showed it to Enzo. 'OK, here we go. Just a T-shirt. Nothing to be worried about.'

With Mauro murmuring instructions behind her, she eased the neck of the shirt over Enzo's head.

'There we go. Now we need to put your hand through here,' she said, indicating the armhole as Enzo shrank away from her. She sat back on her heels, giving him some space. 'I don't need to touch,' she said gently. 'The armhole is right there by your hand. Do you think, when you feel ready, you can get your fingers through it?'

Behind her, Mauro spoke a few words of quiet Italian, and she guessed that he had translated her words. Enzo looked up and met her gaze, but made no signs of moving.

'I can't,' he said.

'You can.' She laid a hand on his uninjured arm. 'I know you can do this.'

Slowly, carefully, he moved his hand into the armhole, and with frequent glances at his face, to make sure that he was OK, Amber eased the rest of the fabric around his elbow, taking some of the weight off the injured limb.

She grabbed a bandage from the first-aid pack and gently wrapped it around the sling, so that the broken arm was pinned to Enzo's chest. He finally let out a sigh of relief as she finished and Amber was relieved to see some colour returning to his face. She replaced the blanket around him, and turned to talk quick and low to Mauro.

'How far to the station?'

'The route we were going to take? Thirty minutes. There's another route that should only take ten, but…'

'But?'

'It's steep.'

'I can manage.'

'I don't doubt it.'

'Oh.' She looked at his cycle. It had never even occurred to her that he had planned their route to take his disability into account. She had got so used to him being able to do anything that she could that she had almost forgotten that his way of seeing the world was different from hers.

'There are a couple of steps. Nothing that you and Enzo wouldn't be able to manage, but I can't get the cycle up them.'

'I can send Mountain Rescue back for you,' she said, and it wasn't until the words left her mouth that she realised that she'd come to a decision.

'I'm not letting you go alone. It's dangerous, Amber.'

She glanced over at Enzo. 'Do you really think he can walk for thirty minutes? Show me on the map. I've a compass on my phone. I can do it.'

They both looked over at Enzo. Although some colour had returned to his face, it was still creased with pain and he was cradling his injured arm like a baby bird.

'He'll have to wait, I'm not letting you go,' Mauro said.

She couldn't suppress a small smile at that. 'We'll be fine. You know it's the right thing. I know that I can do this, and I'll send a team back for you.'

'We…not get lost,' Enzo said from behind them. 'I climb many times.'

'There you are,' she said, leaning in close so that Enzo couldn't hear them. 'Please, I'm going to go quickly. For his sake. I'll see you back at the *funivia* in no time.'

Mauro nodded, knowing that she was right and—more importantly—that they didn't have a choice. He forced a smile, tugging on the front of her jacket. With one firm hand on the nape of her neck and the other on her back, he stole a quick, hard kiss on the lips.

CHAPTER NINE

AMBER PACED THE floor of the *funivia* station, looking again at her watch. Forty-eight minutes had passed since she had left Mauro, alone, on a volcano in zero visibility. She had told him that she was sending Mountain Rescue back for him, and two volunteers from CNSAS, the Sicilian rescue organisation, had headed out to find him. They'd only been half an hour away, he had said. Well, she was going to hold him to that. She was giving him ten more minutes, and then she was going back for him.

Ayisha and Piotr were down at Rifugio Sapienza already, having turned back when they found themselves in poor visibility. Enzo was being cared for by medics, and someone had pushed a cup of hot coffee into her hands but she had batted everyone away, her eyes fixed on the windows, as she waited for Mauro to appear. What would she do if he didn't? How would she feel if he had kissed her goodbye on the mountain, and then he'd had an accident himself? What if he was out there hurt?

He had kissed her.

Despite everything that they had said, despite the fact that their attempts to forget their last kiss had been laughable, he'd gone and done it again.

She looked out of the window once more, hoping for a glimpse of him. Still nothing. She glanced at her watch again. Forty-nine minutes.

Looking over at the mountain rescue team, Amber wondered what they would do if Mauro and the other members of their team didn't turn up. Would they really leave him out there until morning? Well, they might, but she planned on sticking to her word. He could have five more minutes' grace and then she'd be going out there after him.

She started sorting through her pack, working out what extra supplies she would need, when the door to the station flew open, and Mauro wheeled in, the two CNSAS volunteers behind him.

He was bent over the crank of his cycle, his chest heaving, and his face red and shiny from exertion. She dropped her pack and crossed the room, half running.

'Oh, my God, I was just about to come and find you.'

'I'm not—' he was panting, trying to catch his breath '—that late. Had to stop—and check the map.'

She dropped into his lap and framed his face with her hands. 'You had one more minute, I swear.' She leaned in and touched her forehead against his, hesitating for just a second before closing her eyes and brushing her lips against his. Tingles of pleasure shot from where their mouths met down to where his hands had found the small of her back and were holding on tight.

'I'm so glad you're safe,' she breathed, pulling away and then pressing her cheek against his. 'I was worried.'

'So I see.' His hands left her back to wrap tight around her waist. 'But there was no need. I told you.' She stayed still for a few moments, their breathing in sync, as she let her fear subside. But as the adrenaline leached from her system and her heart rate started to slow, she became suddenly self-conscious, nestled in his lap. Glancing over his shoulder, she saw two of the mountain rescue staff grinning at them. She started to slip away, but Mauro's arms pulled her back in tight.

'Don't,' he said, pressing a kiss on her jaw. 'Stay there.'

She looked past him again, and the others in the room were blatantly watching them still.

She smiled, and leaned in close so that they wouldn't be overheard. 'Maybe we should wait until we're alone?'

'And what if I can't?'

She bit her lip, playing with that thought for a moment. What if they couldn't wait? What if they didn't want to? What if she didn't care what anyone else thought?

What if she didn't care that she might get hurt?

'I think we have to try,' she said at last. 'We can talk later, back at the villa.'

He narrowed his eyes as she slipped off his lap. 'You're not interested in taking a risk, are you? Even after we kissed. Even after you started falling for me.'

'I'm n—'

'Don't deny it, Amber. I've seen the way you look at me.' He wheeled closer, back into her personal space, until he barely needed to speak above a whisper. 'I've seen how scared you are, as well. I know that you could only be that afraid because you know that I could hurt you.'

She took a deep breath before she spoke again. 'I've never said that I'm falling for you.' After all she'd decided that she absolutely, definitely wasn't. But the very fact that she'd had to put so much effort into forgetting that one kiss, surely that told her everything that she needed to know about how she felt about Mauro Evans.

So she was falling for him—so what? She wasn't some slave to her libido, or even to her heart. She had to be more careful than that, otherwise she was going to get hurt. It was what Mauro had agreed to—he'd said all along that he didn't want to get involved, so why was he angry about it now?

'But even if I was, what I feel doesn't have to have anything to do with this. Can't you see that? I went with my feelings before, and I got burnt. I don't want that to happen again.'

'And what about this?' he asked, gesturing at the two of them.

She sighed, shaking her head in confusion. 'I need to be sure, Mauro. I need to know that you're not going to hurt me, and I'm afraid your history doesn't exactly work in your favour. What's changed, Mauro? Why would I be any different from all the women you have discarded before me?'

'What's changed? You should know—meeting you, that's what's changed. You're the one who started asking questions about me and Louise. Making me wonder whether I'd got this wrong from the start. And now you're the one who's backing out. Why is that? Is it really because of what Ian did to you? Do you really want to give him that level of control over your life? Let him ruin your future, as well as your past?'

'This has nothing to do with him.' She gritted her teeth, and fought down the anger that always reared its head when she thought of her ex. 'It's the opposite; it's about what I want.'

'And what is that, Amber?'

'I want to not get screwed over, Mauro. You know that I have feelings for you. You know that I can't pretend that that night at Castello Vigneto didn't mean anything. But you're the one who's just pulled a U-turn and I've not had time to catch up. I just need time to think—is that unreasonable? Please, Mauro, it's been a very long day and I don't want to fight. Can we just drop this?'

She watched Mauro take a deep breath, and the lines on his face deepen. He wasn't happy, but she could tell that he didn't want to fight either.

'I want to find out where this could go, Amber. Aren't you curious?'

'Oh, that's what it is, is it? That's what's killing you.' She gave a weary, hollow laugh. 'Here I was thinking it was me that you wanted, but I'm not sticking around because you've just realised that you need to conquer the world of committed relationships next. I'm not going to be your next gold medal, Mauro, because in a month or two, when the shine has worn off, you're going to revert to type and you'll be gone.'

Was she right? Was everything that he was feeling, the pull in his gut every time that he saw her, the need to have her skin against his, the way she filled all his thoughts when they were apart, the way that making her smile made him feel as if he'd just won another gold—was it just novelty?

He couldn't believe that in a week, a month, a year from now, he would feel any different. He didn't have the answers. He didn't know if they *could* make this work. But he knew—he felt—more than anything that walking away now would be something that he would regret for the rest of his life.

He couldn't let Amber just push any mention of what they had aside, as if they didn't matter. But it was clear that her past was holding her back, and if she couldn't come to terms with that, she was never going to give him, give *them* a chance.

One of the park staff called them both over, and explained that they would be able to descend in the cable car. Amber was silent as they were ushered into the *funivia*, and he sent up a silent prayer of thanks that they were alone at last. She had barely said a word since their argument. More than anything, he wanted to reach out and take her hand, to anchor himself to her, but he knew that wouldn't help matters.

'You were amazing out there,' he told her, nodding towards the expanse of thick white fog on the other side of the plastic windows.

A light lit behind her face, and she glowed with a self-confidence he had only seen glimpses of before. 'Thanks. It felt good to help. Maybe I should consider a career change if the show doesn't go well.'

She smiled, but he knew how much her job meant to her. Could she really be so blasé at the thought of losing it?

'There's something I don't understand. Surely your editor wouldn't have hired you if she hadn't thought you were talented. So what's changed?' He asked the question, but it didn't take a genius to guess the answer. Ian, her ex, had happened, and he'd sapped her of her confidence.

'I just couldn't write the way I used to. How could I give romance advice when every time I thought about what Ian had done I grew more convinced that a relationship doesn't bring anything but heartbreak?'

'So you were trying to protect your readers, by telling them not to get involved. The same way you tried to protect yourself. Maybe you're not doing them any favours. Maybe it's time to drop some of those walls, let someone in.'

She looked out of the pod again, out into the clouds, a small smile on her lips.

'Maybe you're right.'

Amber stared in the mirror in her bathroom, a lip crayon stalled halfway to her mouth. Ayisha and her team were waiting for her down on the beach for their last interview, and she knew this one had to be different. She had come out here to save her career, and she still wanted that. She needed her job. But she didn't want to pretend any more. She didn't want to be bitter and defensive, but she didn't want to go back to being the woman she had been before Ian had hurt her either.

Mauro had been right. Since Ian had left she'd given him too much control over her life. First had been the chippy, icy front, and the defensive barriers she'd constructed to stop herself getting hurt. That she'd projected into her work in an attempt to protect others. And then this week pretending it had never happened at all, trying to remember who she'd been before she'd met him, acting out an approximation of that stranger on screen.

She wanted to be the woman who had moved on from that heartache, and come out stronger the other side. She just wanted to be herself.

If she could do that, then she'd be home and free. Well, she'd be home, anyway, waiting to see how the show would be received, whether she would be keeping her job. She lifted her hand and painted some subtle colour onto her lips.

A soft knock on the bathroom door was followed by Mauro poking his head into the room. 'Everything OK?' he asked. 'I think they're ready for us.'

She turned to smile at him. 'Let's do this.'

Mauro came over and gave her a quizzical look. 'What did I miss?'

'What do you mean?'

'You look different.'

She shrugged—and held up the crayon. 'A different colour. I'm impressed. I didn't think you'd notice.'

'No, not that,' he said, reaching up and tilting her chin down. 'No, it's something else. something...*more*. Whatever it is, I like it.'

'Good,' Amber said, replacing the crayon in her make-up bag and zipping it shut. 'Are you ready? Or have you come to pinch my make-up?'

He laughed. 'You are in a good mood. Lead the way, and don't you dare try painting my face.'

'Well,' Julia said, once they were settled out on the loveseat and the camera was rolling. 'That was some dramatic stuff up on the mountain. Can you talk us through what happened?'

Mauro looked so relaxed, Amber thought. And so gorgeous with the sun catching the red in his hair and the gold in his skin.

'Dramatic? It was terrifying!' Amber said, collapsing back in the seat. 'Well, the short story is that we found an injured hiker while we were trekking, and we had to get him to safety.'

'Wow, it sounds like he was lucky you were there,' Julia said after Amber explained about Enzo's broken arm. The presenter leaned forward, eating it up. 'Your trekking experience came in useful, then, Mauro. It's lucky you were there.'

Mauro shrugged and held up his palms, his expression all modesty. 'It did, for the practical stuff, but it was Amber who was really amazing.'

'Oh?' Julia smiled in encouragement. 'Can you tell us more?'

'Well, when we found Enzo, he was understandably distressed—a bit panicked. To start with he didn't want either of us to touch him, but we had to immobilise his broken arm. It was Amber who managed to persuade him to let us help, and then she was so determined to get him quickly to safety that she trekked the last part on her own through dense fog.'

'Wow, pretty brave stuff, Amber.'

'Thanks,' Amber said. 'It didn't feel brave, though. It was just what needed doing. It felt pretty scary actually.'

'But she did it anyway,' Mauro interjected. 'Nothing was going to stop her once she realised what had to be done.'

'And what did you think, when you were watching Amber walk away with Enzo?' Julia had leaned in again, and Amber could see from her expression that she knew that she was on to something, that she'd touched on something potentially explosive.

'I thought she was incredible,' Mauro said simply, looking over and meeting her eye. She was rooted to the spot, blood rushing to her cheeks, making her glow with embarrassment and pride. 'She didn't doubt herself for a second. She just did it.'

He wouldn't let her gaze go, and in his expression she saw everything that they had both been too scared to say out loud. She saw the depth of his feelings for her. She saw herself through his eyes, and she found that she liked the filter—she was the woman who had come through the other side of adversity. She saw a survivor.

Despite Mauro's modesty, she knew that she would never have found safety without his guidance. And he wouldn't have got Enzo to safety without her. It had only worked out because they had worked together. They had both understood what they brought to the situation and had used their gifts accordingly.

As the interview wound down, she felt a frisson of excitement. She still couldn't see how it could work; couldn't see how they could fit a relationship into two lives with no space. But for the first time, she could really see the new her and Mauro clearly. She could see who he really was, past the playboy reputation. And she could see how he felt about her. She didn't know where things were going from here, but she felt for certain that this was the start of something, not the end.

CHAPTER TEN

AMBER SQUEEZED HER headphones a little tighter against her head, trying to block out the noise from the blades of the helicopter.

'It's so… *Loud* doesn't seem the right word. I can *feel* the noise,' she shouted.

'Amazing, isn't it?' Mauro replied over the headsets. 'I love that feeling.'

He had always got a hit of adrenaline from the way that it overwhelmed all his senses—what you could hear was the least of it. His belly vibrated with it. He could practically taste it. And tonight there seemed to be something extra, some new vibration in the air that he hadn't felt before. He glanced across at Amber, who had her hands pressed over her earphones as she looked out of the window.

Not that there was much to see at the moment. The sun had set an hour ago, and the airfield offered little more than runway lights and the windows of the control tower by way of visual interest. All of that would change when they were up in the air, he hoped. He'd been waiting to see Stromboli erupt for nearly a year—during its last great show he'd been on the other side of the world and missed it.

There wasn't room in the cabin for a camera crew, so one of the sports cameras had been rigged up in one corner, so unobtrusive he kept forgetting it was even there. After that interview, he suspected there was a fair bit to say. And they were running out of time. Amber would be flying back to London first thing tomorrow. He felt a dip in his stomach as the helicopter lifted off the ground, and Amber reached for his hand in her excitement.

'Ugh, do you ever get used to that?'

'To what?'

'Hovering,' she shouted, 'just above the Earth like that. It feels weird.'

'Weirder than the enormous jet that we flew out here on?' He laughed at her excitement; her smile was infectious.

'Of course! On the plane you can barely see outside. It's basically a tube carriage with wings and—if you're lucky and fight for the window seat—a marginally better view. This is…this is really *flying*.'

'Maybe I have got a little too used to it.'

When had that happened? he wondered. The last time he'd flown, he was sure that he had had that same tremor of excitement that he'd always felt, but tonight, he'd been distracted. It was Amber. She was the reason, he realised. He'd been more interested in her than the sensations of flying. More interested in the light in her eyes when they'd taken off, the little gasp of breath that she'd given when the skids had left the ground and they'd held just above the Earth, weightless.

Normally he was so excited, waiting for that moment when the aircraft tilted slightly, and the world tipped on its axis, before they were away. For a man who had to exert an enormous amount of energy just getting himself from his bed to his chair in the morning, the freedom he felt in a helicopter was unrivalled. The only thing that came even close was being in the pool. He had already had some flying lessons, with a gadget that adapted the controls for him to operate with his hands. Next year would be the year that he got his licence, he decided. He'd base himself in London for a few months, where he'd taken his first lessons, and get the hours that he needed clocked up.

And maybe see Amber while he was there.

Where had that thought come from? When they were on Etna she'd been as insistent as ever that their kiss had been a mistake, an aberration, and mustn't be repeated. But there had been something in her expression when they had given that interview to Julia that made him think she was having second thoughts. It was what he had been hoping for: that she could see that she could trust him. That he was nothing like her ex. But now he had an inkling that it might have worked, that she might be considering this thing between them after all, his heart started to race.

The pilot's voice broke into the headset, and Mauro snapped back to the present.

'We're just approaching the south side of Stromboli now,' he told them both. 'As you can see, she's pretty lively tonight.'

Rivers of lava were spitting out of the mountain and flowing down the side of the rock, tracks of light and colour in a black night. But they held Mauro's attention for only a few moments. Amber's gaze was fixed out of the helicopter's window, the light of the volcano reflected in her eyes and a look of wonder on her features.

'It's spectacular,' she whispered.

'Beautiful,' Mauro agreed. But he was far

more interested in watching Amber, the way that she pressed her hand against the glass as if she wanted to get closer, to be part of the sky itself.

As the helicopter turned, Amber turned too, to look out of the other side, and her body pressed up against his arm in the close confines of the cabin. The heat from her skin nearly burned him, as if he had been plunged into one of those rivers of fire.

The experience was all her.

He had been anticipating this experience for months, since long before he had met Amber, but he knew with unbridled certainty now that it would not have been complete without her. Nothing could compare to the experience of seeing this vision with her by his side. An emptiness opened up in his chest, and he wondered how many other experiences had been lacking for want of her company. He thought that he had travelled the planet to see its most incredible sights. He had kept moving, constantly looking for the next big adventure, always wanting to better the last. Would they all have had this extra sparkle, the extra intensity? There was something about tonight that didn't feel real. It recalled those days after his accident, when the doctors had thrown every drug they could at him to help control the nerve pain.

He'd never dabbled with drugs recreationally, and now he knew why. Because once you had something that heightened every sensation, made every colour brighter, every emotion more intense, it was hard to know how you came back from that. How you could go back to the life you led before. Next time he saw a volcano erupt, or a glacier slide into arctic waters, or jumped an epic wave on his jet ski, would the experience be dulled by the lack of Amber to share it with?

Sweat broke out on his forehead as panic started to set in. He had tried having a relationship before, and he had failed. His life didn't work with anyone else in it.

A huge plume of fire shot from the island, and Amber grabbed for his hand, squeezing it tight. And just like that, the pounding of his heart stopped, his chest relaxed, and he let out the breath that he was holding. He didn't have all the answers, and it didn't matter. Because if she was willing to give this a go, they would work it out together.

He would make it work: for her. He would compromise: for her. He would find time and space in his life. For her. It was all for her. She was the woman who made his world bright, his heart beat stronger, his laugh come louder. He knew, deep in his gut, that he wouldn't have shared this experience with anyone else.

Amber looked him in the eye.

'Are you OK?' she asked.

He had to convince her to give him a shot. She was scared, and she had every right to be after what she had been through, but he couldn't give up on them yet. His eyes dropped to their clasped hands and he smiled. 'Better than OK,' he said. 'I'm great.'

She opened her mouth to speak, but then glanced over at their pilot.

'Giorgio, can you give us some privacy?' Mauro asked him. The man flicked a switch on his headset and gave them a thumbs up.

'I was just going to say—' she started to speak and he dropped his gaze to watch her slide her fingers sensuously between his '—that this is just about the most incredible thing I've ever seen.'

The husky tone of her voice and the sight of her hand in his hit him straight in the gut. If this woman was the one, life could definitely be a lot worse.

Shutting out his worries with the closing of his eyes, he leaned towards her. Their last kiss had been gentle, hesitant. This was one fired by the lava spewing beneath them. He grabbed a handful of her hair, pulling her closer as his lips moved towards hers, heat and passion flowing through his body.

She drew in a sharp breath, and for a second he froze, scared beyond measure that she was about to push him away, but then her body went supple and relaxed beside him as she pulled him across to her, and he heard a low moan of desire in his headset. Her lips parted, and her hand moved to slide sensuously up his thigh—he dropped his eyes to watch, and the sight of that seductive caress sent a shiver up his spine. But it wasn't enough. He moved her hand from the dead zone on his thigh to a spot where he could feel the warmth of her fingers, and then he closed the distance between them and took her lips in a searing kiss.

Her hands were in his hair, they were dancing across his shoulders, teasing at the hem of his shirt and pulling at the buttons. Her mouth was on his, demanding and passionate, testing the limits of his patience and his control. And her moans and breaths were in his ears, magnified by the headset so they could be heard even over the thrumming hum of the helicopter blades.

He cursed the safety harnesses that pinned them to their seats, wishing that he could snap her buckle open and drag her into his lap. With her straddling him, there was no telling what they could get up to. But as the helicopter swooped around reality hit him and he remembered where they were, and that they weren't alone. Thank God he'd thought to tell Giorgio to turn his headset off.

With a strength of mind he hadn't known he possessed, he pulled away from her. She wouldn't meet his eye as they both caught their breath, so he snuck a sweet kiss high on her cheekbone, bringing a smile to her lips.

'To be continued,' he said with a grin, before tapping their pilot on the shoulder. 'Ready to head back to base, *amico*.'

Once they were back on the ground, Giorgio gave him a hand getting back into his chair. 'Thanks for letting me borrow the heli,' Giorgio said in English as Mauro stretched his arm to shake hands.

'Any time. Thanks for the ride.'

'Wait,' Amber said as Mauro's driver took them down dark Sicilian lanes. 'You let him borrow it? The helicopter's yours? You know I forget sometimes that you're the guy who can casually go out and buy a helicopter. Can you fly it?'

'Yes and no,' he replied, though his fingers were caressing her knee, and every so often wandering further afield. But she couldn't let this rest. People she knew just didn't *have* helicopters. She couldn't even afford a car. 'I'm working towards my licence. I just need to log some more hours.'

She didn't ask *how* he flew, given that she'd already seen him driving a specially adapted Range Rover. You could adapt pretty much anything, she guessed, if you had enough money and motivation. She closed her eyes and leaned back against him, her whole body focussed now on those fingertips tracing circles on the sensitive skin at the backs of her knees, and the soft skin of her thighs. Something had happened while they were in the air. She couldn't put her finger on what, but the way Mauro had looked at her—equal parts passion and fear—made her nervous.

She opened a bottle of Prosecco when they got back to the villa and carried it outside with a couple of glasses. Mauro was waiting for her on a lounger by the pool. She sat beside him, her elbows propped on her knees and her arms tight in against her body. It was ridiculous, really, to feel shy after what they had just shared. He reached for her hand and threaded his fingers through hers. She wasn't sure what she had been expecting of him, but, after their passionate kiss in the helicopter, it hadn't been this quiet contemplation.

'That was pretty incredible,' he said simply.

Was he referring to the helicopter? The volcano? Or the kiss? It was the 'but' in his voice that gave it away. He was definitely talking about the kiss. Oh, God, were they going to be sensible and reason their way out of this—again? She had been so carried away by the fireworks and the helicopter and the kiss, all their concerns hadn't seemed to matter any more. And once they'd landed, she'd expected them to flood right back in, but it seemed they'd left them up there. All that had landed was her and Mauro, two people who liked each other, who both seemed pretty keen to see where that might go.

'Mauro, I don't—'

'But,' he went on, 'I think we should give ourselves some time to think about what we want.' He reached for her hands, and held them tight in his own.

'You know how I feel about you. I think you're incredible. You're talented and you're kind, and you're beautiful. And, God, this new confidence you've found from somewhere is so sexy it's nearly killing me. I want to find a way for us to make this work. But you've been telling me all week that you don't want to get hurt again, and I think it's the right thing to do to think about this properly.'

She wanted him—so much. She wanted to drag him into the villa, into bed, and show him just how much. She reached for him again, but he wheeled back a fraction, just far enough that he could reach up and frame her face with his hands. 'You know, I'm really hoping that I'm not going to regret this. But I need you to think about this, to be sure. Because if you come to me, Amber, and tell me you want me, I'm not sure I'm ever going to let you go.'

'So what do we do now?' she asked, her body burning in frustration as it realised it wasn't going to get what she wanted tonight. But she could wait a few weeks, if that was what Mauro needed.

'Well, I don't know about you, but I'm going for the world's coldest shower.'

CHAPTER ELEVEN

IT HAD BEEN six long weeks since she had seen Mauro, as he had kissed her goodbye on the terrace of his villa. He had had to fly straight to New York to take care of some business, he had said, and wouldn't be back in London for several weeks at least.

And then a month had passed, and more, with no word from him. And she'd braced herself for the fact that maybe she'd misunderstood what had happened that last night. Here she was in the make-up room of the TV studios, with less than an hour to go until she was on screen, and she hadn't heard a word from him since she had left his villa. A small, tinsel-bedecked TV in the corner of the room was showing what was happening out in the studio, and the knot of fear and nerves in her belly was growing larger and larger.

She'd thought at the time that their last kiss had been a promise, a commitment of more to come. But perhaps it had been goodbye. A curl of embarrassment started in her stomach and radiated out to her skin. What would the production team have done with the footage of those last days in Sicily? The heartfelt conversations they had had on Etna, and the awkward silences in the interviews that had followed, not to mention the kisses at the cable-car station and in the helicopter. It hadn't been until the next day that she'd remembered that there had been a camera in the corner of the cabin.

It would be fodder for an explosive reunion, she supposed.

She'd thought that she might have bumped into Mauro by now, or that at least they'd see each other in the green room before they went on air, but she'd just been told that that definitely wouldn't be happening. They wouldn't lay eyes on each other again until they were on screen. Maximum drama, Ayisha had said. Maximum humiliation was just as likely.

Amber sat in the green room and closed her eyes, trying to block out the streams of conversation flowing around her. She tried to take a deep breath, but the sparkling, sequinned dress that the wardrobe department had thought was suitably festive had other ideas.

Even if Mauro had decided that he didn't want to be with her, she couldn't be sorry that she'd gone on the date. Finding a man like Mauro had been incredible. But finding herself again—that was a miracle. Something she could only ever be grateful for, even if she never saw him again. She hadn't expected to lose her heart to him, but she'd done it all the same.

She'd known it on the plane, wishing he were beside her.

She'd known it when she'd lain alone in her bed that night, thinking of Mauro's arms, how delicious they'd feel wrapped around her.

She'd known it when she'd arrived at the studios earlier that day, remembering the first time that she'd met him. The flip of her stomach at the sound of his voice as she'd remembered seeing him soaking wet by the side of a pool.

She'd fallen for him. And she wanted him—even though it frightened her.

He was worth the risk.

Like the London drizzle after the Sicilian sunshine, everything in her life had seemed grey and dull since she had returned from their date. She wanted the heat and the spark that only came from being with him. From sharing their experiences. From seeing things together.

And if she'd managed to convince him that she didn't want him, then she was going to have to undo the damage herself. If she wanted him, she was going to have to make it happen.

But what was she meant to say, how was she meant to act with the whole country watching? She was just going to have to tell him, she realised. Tell him that she still wanted him, that she loved him, and hope that he still felt the same. Be honest with herself, and with him. And if he rejected her? Then he rejected her. She couldn't control him, or his feelings. All she could do was share hers with him and hope that that was enough.

Ayisha appeared at the door of the green room with her tablet computer.

'All right, Amber, we'll be live in about fifteen minutes. Anything you need to ask before we get started?'

Amber shook her head. It was too late for second thoughts now.

The studio lights were dazzlingly bright, as she waited out of view of the cameras. The set had been dressed for Christmas, and fairy lights glinted and twinkled, reflected off the silver glitter of the decorations and icicles, and in the pillowy white of the fake snow.

The heat of the lights on her skin reminded her of watching Mount Stromboli erupt from the window of the helicopter. Just the memory of that night was enough to push her forward to centre stage when she heard her cue, when a very large part of her wanted to run and hide, away from the intrusive glare of the cameras and audience.

'Please welcome... Amber Harris...and Mauro Evans!'

She stumbled towards the couch in the middle of the stage with her eyes fixed on the enormous Christmas tree just behind Julia, too afraid to look at Mauro, who she knew would be coming in from the opposite side. She needed to keep herself together. If she looked at him, she knew that she'd lose her composure—she just had to hold her nerve a little longer.

Once she was centre stage, the long sequinned dress no longer felt out of place. The lights were winking and shining off her the same as they were from the decorations. The Christmas tree was at least twenty feet tall, with baubles as big as grapefruits of glass and silver and glitter; candles burned on every surface and Julia was waiting for her in an enormous wingback chair upholstered in white velvet, beside a matching couch, just big enough for two.

It was a fantasy Christmas wonderland, and at its centre she felt intoxicated by it.

And there, still with his ice-white shirt, was Mauro. The audience broke into enthusiastic applause, and at last Amber risked a glance at him from beneath her lashes. She couldn't risk looking at him full-on. Not yet. She closed her eyes completely as she leant in to kiss him on the cheek, just as she'd been briefed by Ayisha. Just like that first time, when she'd done the same thing, almost on this very spot.

The closed eyes didn't help. They did nothing to block out the feel of his rough cheek against her smooth skin. Or to block out his scent, so delicious, so familiar, with that hint of sea salt that was as much a part of him as his charm.

She'd not swum since she'd been back in London. She couldn't face the reminder of him. Of the electric crackle of chemistry between them, a spark that held so much promise. If they have the courage to pursue it. Eventually she couldn't put it off any longer and, just for a moment, she drank him in. That dark red hair, its wildness not quite subdued by whatever product had been dragged through it. The white shirt still effortlessly chic, and perfectly highlighting his golden skin. And his eyes. Green, and deep, and full of emotion.

Not the cheeky twinkle that had flirted with her that first night that they met, but wells of something deeper and more serious. Secrets hidden from their audience, and something hidden from her as well. The last time that she'd seen him, he had laid all his cards on the table. Had told her everything that he felt for her, and asked for honesty and truth in return. And now here he was, guarded. Hiding something.

'Look at these two, don't they make such a gorgeous couple?' Julia turned to the audience with a sparkling smile while a member of the production team encouraged the audience to clap and cheer. 'We're all so happy to have you both here with us. So, before the commercial break our audience saw that magic moment when you surprised us all, Mauro, and picked Amber to accompany you to your beautiful home in Sicily, but, just for you two, let's see again where all this started.'

While the VT of their first meeting showed, Mauro moved from his chair to the couch beside her, but he refused to meet her eye. She still had no idea what he was thinking.

She watched their first awkward meeting and felt a blush rise on her cheeks. She was so guarded. So prickly—she remembered, of course, but what she hadn't seen then was the look on Mauro's face with each of her answers, entertained and intrigued. Proof, right in front of her eyes, of how badly her plan to push him away had been doomed to failure from the beginning.

'And now, what we've all been dying to see.

How did you two get on when we sent you away for a week of sun, sand and…ahem…?'

'Jet-skiing?' Mauro supplied.

She breathed a sigh of relief at the sound of familiar humour in his voice. Maybe this would be OK after all. But then her spine grew straighter and straighter as they watched their week together unfolding on screen. Some moments when she'd known the cameras were rolling—and then some she hadn't.

They'd been there, somewhere behind them, when Mauro had caught her toes with his wheelchair in the airport, and captured the moment when he'd pulled her into his lap. Her cheeks warmed and her breath caught when she remembered how close she'd come to kissing him. How she'd been overwhelmed by the heat of his body, the way that his chest and his arms had so totally engulfed her.

She risked a glance at Mauro, and their eyes met as he looked across at her for just a moment. A shared smile melted some of the frost between them.

And then she'd leapt off his lap like a scalded cat, and just like that the moment between them had been lost.

Those first couple of days in Sicily, they'd caught lingering glances and shared smiles. The end of that first swimming lesson, when she'd been so aware of Mauro's eyes on her body. She had felt more exposed that day, with one man watching, than she did now, with her swimsuit-clad body broadcast to the nation.

God knew, the footage made no secret of where the producers thought this story was heading. They didn't have the money shot, so to speak—no smoking gun, but there was plenty of circumstantial evidence.

And then the fog descended—literally and metaphorically—during their hike up Etna; and the fires raged on Stromboli, and a great big question mark hung over where they were going next. The producers had been kind—it could have been a lot worse—and not a shot of that kiss in the helicopter was broadcast. But it was clear what direction this interview was going to take—they were obviously hoping for Christmas fireworks.

'So then, you two. I think we saw some sparks flying there. What's been happening since that was shot?'

'Well, Julia, I'm sorry if this comes as a disappointment…' ah, that voice with its rich mixture of Welsh and Italian; a combination that shouldn't work but in reality was dangerously seductive '…but I've actually been in New York since that was filmed. So this is the first time we've seen each other since.'

'Oh, how exciting!' Julia declared with a clap of her hands—Amber admired her ability to sell a lie. If she'd had half her talent, this whole charade would have been a hell of a lot easier from start to finish. 'Reunited right here, with us. Tell me, then, Amber, what's it like seeing Mauro again?'

She opened her mouth to speak, but found that her tongue was dry and her lips paralysed. A prickle of sweat beaded in her palms and she shifted on the couch, willing herself to speak.

It had to be now. If she didn't tell him how she felt tonight, then this could all be over. If this show hadn't been booked, maybe she never would have seen him again. And if she couldn't even speak, she was going to lose him—and deserve it.

'Uh, well, it's…nice.' Nice? She wanted to scream at herself. After everything, that was all she could come up with—nice?

But what if she laid out her every emotion in heart-rending detail, and then he turned her down? If she could just have a clue as to what he was feeling she knew that she could do better. She opened her mouth to try again, but Julia was already jumping in with another question.

'OK… So, Amber thinks it's "nice" to see you, Mauro. How are *you* feeling seeing Amber again?'

He glanced across at Amber, and she could feel her cheeks warm. 'Well, it's not often that she's lost for words. I'm pretty surprised by that.'

Still he evaded her eye.

'Well, you two are playing your cards pretty close to your chests.' Julia raised her eyebrows theatrically towards the audience and got a ripple of laughter and applause in response. 'How about we look at this another way: have you got plans to see each other again?'

She could see that Mauro was about to speak, but there were things she needed to say before they could answer that question. She laid her hand on his, and felt a shot of heat and electricity straight to her heart. She drew in a steadying breath and spoke.

'Mauro, wait.'

Finally, *finally* he turned and properly held her gaze. As his green eyes bore into hers, she could see surprise. But that wasn't all. There was still a spark there, a look so familiar from their time together in Sicily that it gave her the courage to speak on. From the corner of her eye she saw genuine shock on Julia's face at the way that she had silenced Mauro, and rushed to fill the vacuum with the speech that she'd started rehearsing weeks ago. If she wanted Mauro to know how she felt then she had to tell him—and now. If she waited, she'd lose her nerve, and might never have the opportunity again.

'Look, Mauro. I know what I said before, when we were at Etna…' She glanced up at Julia, wondering if Mauro was going to make her spell it out, air all their dirty laundry. His face showed no emotion, and she knew that she had no choice but to lay it all on the line. 'I was scared. We both know it. I was terrified because of when I got hurt before, and I was worried that it was going to happen again with you, and I let that keep me away. Because you were right, Mauro. We both know that you were. I'm falling for you. Damn it, I've fallen. I've fallen headfirst, stupidly, recklessly in love with you.'

Her words were met with a shocked silence. In her peripheral vision she could see Julia staring at her in shock. But she was distracted by that for only a fraction of a second. She couldn't drag her eyes from Mauro, who was looking at her with careful regard. She wasn't sure what she had been expecting, but this sangfroid was her worst nightmare. If he'd been repulsed, told her to forget it—she would have been devastated. If he'd declared his own feelings she would have been elated. But this—this meant that she had to go on. She drew herself up a little taller, pushed her shoulders back, opening up her chest, and started speaking again.

'That week with you was the best week of my life. Even though I spent half the time pretty terrified, and a lot of it mad either with you or myself. And Etna was a bit of a disaster, and you kept asking me to be brave about my feelings for you and I couldn't do it. It's just so incredible to have found someone that makes me want to risk all that again—risk *feeling* again—

that I don't want to give it up. I don't want to give *you* up, Mauro.'

She waited again. That was it. That was all that she had to say, and if it wasn't enough… Well, there would be nothing she could do other than accept it. Lick her wounds. Hibernate. Work out how she was going to rebuild her life again. Because even if Mauro didn't still want her, she wouldn't go back to where she was before she'd met him. It wasn't fair to him, wasn't fair to what she'd learnt in their week together to act as if it had never happened. Even if he wanted to forget the whole thing, she wouldn't. She'd never forget that week, and she'd never forget the man who made her realise that she could be whole again, even after her heart had been broken.

But now she had said everything. She couldn't force him to want her. All she could do now was wait and see.

She looked long and hard into his eyes.

'Of course I still want you.' The light and

sparkle was back in his face, and she could feel the heat crackling between them in a way that made her realise how cold she had been ever since they'd got back. 'What kind of guy do you think I am?'

'Oh, my God!' She grabbed his face and kissed him hard on the lips. 'You are so infuriating! You've been avoiding me for weeks and you choose now—'

He smacked her a kiss back, and then dropped his voice until it was little more than a breath. 'You wouldn't want me all biddable, would you?' he murmured and a shot of heat went straight from her lips to between her legs.

He was right, of course. He wouldn't be the man that she loved if he had been anything other than absurdly confident that everything would go his way. She leaned in again for another kiss, when a melodramatic throat-clearing behind him reminded her that they were still on live TV. A rush of blood heated her cheeks, and she knew that they must be blazing red.

'So it seems like we've got some catching up to do here!' Julia declared. 'Are you going to fill us in on what's been going on?'

She looked across at Mauro. She didn't want to use him, to exploit their relationship, but they both knew that she had got into this because she needed to improve her image, and now they had the perfect opportunity to do that, just by sharing their happiness. But it wasn't just her decision to make.

'Well, I think we can just put it down to me being irresistible,' Mauro said with a smug look on his face. 'I've said all along that it was inevitable, you know. She couldn't help but fall in love with me.'

Amber laughed and leaned in close as his arm wrapped around her shoulders. At last. At last she had him exactly where she wanted him. At last, she was exactly where she wanted to be. 'Well, there's not a lot I can say to counter that, is there,' she said, 'given that I was absolutely hopeless at resisting?'

Julia looked on them indulgently for a second, before glancing across at Ayisha, who was mouthing something from behind the camera. 'But back to the interview… Amber seems to think that you've been avoiding her, Mauro? Surely that can't be true.'

'Yeah, I noticed that,' he said. 'I haven't—I swear. I had work in New York and then something came up that demanded my personal attention in Mexico. I only had time to fit in one last errand in London before I came to the studio, so I've genuinely not had a minute of free time since I last saw her. But seriously, Julia, I owe you, big time. If you hadn't invited me to come on here, I wouldn't have met the woman of my dreams, the woman I want to spend the rest of my life with, if she'll have me.'

Amber's jaw dropped open. The rest of his life? She'd been so elated that he'd not just rejected her on live TV she hadn't even thought about where this might be going past that first kiss.

'The rest of your life?' Her voice shook as

she asked the question, but she had to do it. She had to know how he felt about commitment, whether they were just empty words or whether he actually meant them. About the fear that he might be missing out on something else. She'd seen genuine panic in his eyes when they had been growing closer on the island, and she couldn't quite believe that he could have such a complete turnaround.

Mauro reached into his jacket pocket, but Amber was distracted by a squeal from Julia—the woman looked as if she'd just been slapped. Or told she had a winning lottery ticket. She wasn't sure which.

'Julia, are you—?' Amber started. 'Oh, my God.' At the sight of the small velvet box in Mauro's hand, the words caught in her throat, and she found that she couldn't carry on.

'Mauro…'

'Amber,' he replied. His voice steadier than hers. 'Do you think you can see past the fact that you've told me more than once, in no uncertain terms, that you don't want to get involved with me, and the fact that I was such an idiot it took me nearly a whole week to realise that I can't live without you *and* the fact that I told you that I absolutely, definitely, wouldn't ask you to get involved with me…' As he took a breath a hush descended on the studio.

'Would you do me the very great honour of marrying me?'

The silence seemed to expand within her as the attention and expectation of every person in the room became fixed on her, and on her answer.

Can you trust him?

That little voice in her head was still there. Mauro or no Mauro, she hadn't managed to silence it completely. She hadn't meant to fall in love. Not with him, this playboy who had told her straight that he was never in it for the long haul.

All around her was snow and ice and light, all

of it beautiful, all of it fake. This set was a fantasy, an illusion. Only one thing in it was real.

As she looked up into his eyes she could feel the connection between them, feel that their souls had somehow, in the heat and steam and chaos of a volcano, melted and become one. That it was as impossible to separate them now as it would be to prise the lava from those hillsides.

Her gaze was locked onto Mauro, and just as she was about to speak she saw a tiny crease line his forehead, and that was what did for her. That tiny crack of self-doubt, the softness that she knew was inside him, hiding inside this crazy man who had no fear, even at the thought of proposing marriage live on air.

'I'd be crazy not to,' she said with a smile. 'Yes, Mauro, I'd very much like to marry you.'

Mauro let out a whoop as he wrapped his arms tight around her waist and dragged her unceremoniously onto his lap.

'I promise you I'm going to make you the happiest woman in the world for the rest of your life,' he said as he opened the ring box.

Amber gasped at the sight of the stone, blazing orange and pink in a band of icy platinum and diamonds.

'It's a Mexican fire opal,' Mauro said. 'It reminded me of—'

But she cut him off with a kiss before he could finish the sentence.

'It's beautiful,' she said, coming up for air. 'Absolutely beautiful.'

She leaned in to kiss him again, and for a few long moments the rest of the world disappeared, forced out of her consciousness by the volume of her shock and delight. Gradually, though, the silence of their little bubble faded, and reality started to crash back into Amber's world.

'Congratulations, you beautiful pair,' Julia gushed. 'When's the wedding—and where? I'd better be on the guest list, because if I'm not then I'll be gatecrashing!'

Mauro and Amber both laughed.

'I think it's a little early to be announcing a venue, but I promise you we'll let you know.'

From the corner of her eye Amber spotted Ay-isha still gesticulating wildly, and she guessed that Mauro's little stunt had taken the show ca-reering off course. Well, if you couldn't bend your schedule for a little romance, then what were any of us doing here at all?

Julia was still gushing at them both, and Amber noticed a tear had escaped the corner of her eye as she pressed her hands into Mauro's with more congratulations. But Mauro was ex-tracting his hands, gently, she noticed. And then one giant paw had enclosed her fingers.

'Now, if you don't mind, Julia, I think my fi-ancée and I need to be going.'

Without another word he had shoved her off his lap, moved to his chair, and grabbed her hand. He wheeled off the studio stage, only pausing at the last minute and giving the show's signature wave, and then they were behind the scenery, and away from the public glare.

From the corner of her eye, Amber noticed a runner approaching them, but when Mauro's fingers curled into her hair and pulled her down for a kiss, her eyes closed and the world melted away.

The kiss burned through her with the intensity of a wildfire. But a niggling thought dampened the flames.

'You're sure, though, Mauro. Because I know you, and I remember everything you said in Sicily. I can't go into this lightly. If I'm getting married, it's going to be for ever. I need to know that that's what you want too.'

Mauro loosened his arms from around her waist, and she stood, suddenly unsure. Wondering whether she wanted to hear what he had to say. Maybe she should have just gone along with it, regardless. Maybe she could learn to be happy in the moment, as Mauro was, rather than worrying about what their future might bring.

But no. She girded herself, and stuck to her principles. If she was going to make a commitment, she had to mean it, and she had to know that Mauro meant it too.

He reached for her hands, preventing her from withdrawing any more.

'Amber, *amore mio*, I've never been more sure about anything. I love you. These past few weeks have been hell without you, but I owed it to you to think it through. To give you time to think about things too. That day after the mountain everything was so…heated. It wasn't the time to make big decisions.'

'Whereas live TV…'

'That bit wasn't exactly planned. I was going to wait until later, but then you said what you did and I couldn't help it. I want you. I want us, and I want it to start right now.'

He meant it. There was no doubting the expression on his face when he looked at her, no mistaking the hope and fear and doubt in his eyes.

She leaned in for another kiss, soft and gentle this time, a promise of everything that was to come.

'Right now?'

He nodded.

'Then you'd better take me home.'

EPILOGUE

AMBER THREW ANOTHER log into the fire, and watched as the flames licked up the side, yellow, orange and red all dancing in the grate.

'Home,' she'd said to Mauro. 'Take me home.'

She'd not given any thought to the word as it passed her lips, and it was only when they had climbed into the waiting car that she'd even questioned where they were going.

'My place?' he'd asked.

She'd agreed without thinking about it. Of course his place. What were they going to do? Huddle round the solitary space heater in her flat? She'd spent that night at his penthouse suite in Mayfair, and then another. And another. In the weeks since the show aired she'd only gone back to her flat for clothes and basic supplies.

And then his friend had lent him this house for Christmas—it was only a few streets away from his hotel, but their first Christmas together warranted somewhere more festive, he'd said. And she couldn't fault the house on the festive front. The tree in the hallway, lit with flickering LED candles, looked as if it could have been in that exact spot for a hundred years. Garlands weaved between the spindles of the banisters, and a huge green wreath greeted guests at the front door opposite the gated park. Even the British weather had delivered, and she could see snow gathering on the windowpanes.

The floorboards were original, sanded and waxed to a perfect glow, and covered with luxurious rugs, plush underfoot. And under her back, she thought. And her elbow, as she lifted herself to look at Mauro, who was still snoozing beside her on the floor. She pulled the blanket up higher over them, and traced her fingers across Mauro's chest, outlining the pectoral muscle and drifting through the auburn-tinted hairs.

'Mmm…' he said, his voice still full of sleep. 'Are you trying to wake me up?'

'Maybe.' She smiled and glanced at the clock, just as the minute hand hit the twelve. 'Merry Christmas,' she said, dropping a kiss on his cheek.

His eyes flew open and he pushed himself up, toppling her off him in the process. 'It's midnight already?' he asked, looking flustered. 'How did that happen?'

She wrapped the throw around herself, taken aback by Mauro's change in mood.

'Uh, well, you suggested that we get a brandy and come and sit down here by the fire, see in Christmas morning, and then you said…'

His face softened, and then broke into a grin. 'I know. I remember; I'm sorry.' He kissed her, a smile still on his lips. 'I'm just excited.'

'About Christmas Day?' She laughed and leaned in against his shoulder. 'You big kid.'

'Don't get too comfy.' He pulled the throw away from her, leaving her chilly, and he reached for his shirt, discarded beside them, and wrapped it around her shoulders. 'I need you to do me a favour.'

'Now?'

'Yes, now. It's Christmas, it has to be now.'

Amber pushed her arms into the sleeves, and stood with an air of resignation. She knew that once he'd got an idea in his head, it was impossible to change his mind.

'My jacket,' he said. 'Over the back of the chair in the hall. There's an envelope in the inside pocket. Can you grab it for me?'

She did as he asked, and when she got back to the rug, he was sitting up, his back against the couch, the throw blanket tucked over his lap. 'Come back in,' he said, holding up one corner, and she crawled in beside him, nestling into his heat again.

'Here.' She handed him the envelope, curiosity starting to niggle at her.

But he handed the envelope straight back to her.

'Merry Christmas,' he said.

She took the envelope from him and turned it over in her hands before she opened it slowly, carefully, with half an eye still on Mauro's face. He looked nervous, she thought. And excited. And all of a sudden she was nervous too, about what she was going to find in that envelope. Was she going to like it?

She pulled out the sheaf of papers and started reading. Then skipped to the next page. And the next. She didn't understand. How could he...? He couldn't have...

'A house, Mauro?'

'This house!' he declared, kissing her on the lips. 'Merry Christmas, Amber. I hope you like it.'

'Oh, my God.' She couldn't speak past the

orange-sized lump in her throat. She forced it down, and tried to string a sentence together.

'Mauro, I can't accept this house. This is crazy. You've bought me a *house*. In *Mayfair*.'

He smiled, still apparently not seeing that there was anything weird about this situation.

'Look,' he said, tucking her hair behind her ear, 'I know what happened to you before. I know how much your independence means to you. But I want us to be together. I want us to live together.' He dropped another kiss on her lips. 'Most of all, I want you to feel safe, secure. That's why I bought you this house, but I hope you'll let me live with you.'

She couldn't take her eyes from the deeds. From the space where her name was in bold black ink. The owner of this house. Mauro was right. For nearly two years she'd been living in fear of ending up with nowhere to call home, and now he was telling her that she would never have to feel that again.

Except now...everything was different. She

didn't just want a roof over her head. She wanted a home, and she knew that a house could never be that again without Mauro there too.

'Of course you'll live with me,' she said. 'But this…this is too much.' He opened his mouth to speak, but she had to have her say. 'I want us to live together, Mauro. With both our names on the deeds.'

'But I thought that you'd want—'

'And it was so thoughtful of you. But let's do this together. Take this leap together. I want to go into this marriage knowing we're equals. I trust you. I love you.'

He leaned down and kissed her hard, pulling her onto his lap and wrapping his arms around her. 'I love you so much,' he said. 'And we're going to make this such a happy home. Merry Christmas, Amber.'

'Merry Christmas, Mauro,' she whispered against his lips.

She relaxed into his body, the fire, the brandy and the heat of her fiancé warming her to her bones, and she knew without question that this was only the first of a lifetime of Christmases they'd welcome in this room.

* * * * *

MILLS & BOON®

Large Print – April 2017

A Di Sione for the Greek's Pleasure
Kate Hewitt

The Prince's Pregnant Mistress
Maisey Yates

The Greek's Christmas Bride
Lynne Graham

The Guardian's Virgin Ward
Caitlin Crews

A Royal Vow of Convenience
Sharon Kendrick

The Desert King's Secret Heir
Annie West

Married for the Sheikh's Duty
Tara Pammi

Winter Wedding for the Prince
Barbara Wallace

Christmas in the Boss's Castle
Scarlet Wilson

Her Festive Doorstep Baby
Kate Hardy

Holiday with the Mystery Italian
Ellie Darkins

0317 Rom LP

MILLS & BOON®

Large Print – May 2017

A Deal for the Di Sione Ring
Jennifer Hayward

The Italian's Pregnant Virgin
Maisey Yates

A Dangerous Taste of Passion
Anne Mather

Bought to Carry His Heir
Jane Porter

Married for the Greek's Convenience
Michelle Smart

Bound by His Desert Diamond
Andie Brock

A Child Claimed by Gold
Rachael Thomas

Her New Year Baby Secret
Jessica Gilmore

Slow Dance with the Best Man
Sophie Pembroke

The Prince's Convenient Proposal
Barbara Hannay

The Tycoon's Reluctant Cinderella
Therese Beharrie